Shaking in the Shack

Books in the *YaYa & YoYo* Series

Sliding Into the New Year

Shaking in the Shack

Praise for *YaYa & YoYo: Shaking in the Shack*

"In this enjoyable second volume in the *YaYa & YoYo* children's book series, Dori Weinstein does a beautiful job of teaching Jewish values, from respecting nature and animals, to caring for each other. Readers will enjoy the playful banter and antics of the close-knit and fun-loving Silver family, and will learn more about Judaism's rich history as we gather under the Sukkah together."

Gail Rosenblum
Columnist, Minneapolis Star Tribune
Author of *A Hundred Lives Since Then: Essays on Motherhood, Marriage, Mortality and More*

"*Shaking in the Shack* brings us another fun romp with YaYa and YoYo and the Silver family! Dori Weinstein portrays the holiday of Sukkot as a joyful celebration of family, friends, and caring for others. The relatable and likable characters demonstrate healthy, positive relationships among friends, siblings and between adults and children. The threads from the first book are a nice link and book two also stands well on its own. Packed with positive messages, *Shaking in the Shack* is a great addition to Jewish middle-grade literature."

Amy Ariel
Jewish educator and Author of *Friends Forever*

"*Shaking in the Shack* is an engaging story for young readers. It is really exciting to have characters in a series that our Jewish young readers can identify with and learn from."

Judy Miller, M.S.
Head of School, Columbus Jewish Day School
Columbus, Ohio

"More adventure. More learning. More fun. So glad to see YaYa and YoYo returning. Another young adult hit by Dori Weinstein. I can't wait to see what the kids will be doing for Hanukkah!"

"Another winner from Dori Weinstein! Like her first book, the story unfolds so naturally, you don't realize how much you're absorbing about Jewish culture and practice. Dori perfectly captures the tween voice with YaYa and YoYo."

Shaking in the Shack

Dori Weinstein

Five Flames Press

Copyright © 2013 by Dori Weinstein

YaYa & YoYo: Shaking in the Shack
First edition—April 2013
Five Flames Press

www.yayayoyo.com

Cover illustration by Ann D. Koffsky
Cover Design by Ilana Weinstein
Cover Graphics by Ward Barnett
Editor: Leslie Martin

ISBN: 0-9890193-0-6
ISBN-13: 978-0-9890193-0-9

10 9 8 7 6 5 4 3 2 1

For Gary, Ari, Ilana, and Eitan

No matter where we find our shelter,
Be it a house, a tent, or a sukkah,
You make it Home

Contents

1

Let's Get This Party Started

You'd think that my twin sister was a presidential candidate waiting for election results to come in, the way she paced in the foyer. I could almost imagine the "Ellie Silver for President" campaign button on her shirt.

"Joel, where are they?" she asked as if I had the answer. Then, without actually waiting for a reply, she chanted, "Where are they, where are they, where are they?" in an anxious whisper while wearing a path in the hardwood floor.

It was Thursday night, October eighth, Ellie's eleventh birthday, and she was freaking out because her friends hadn't arrived for her sleepover yet. She was able to have her party on a weeknight because we didn't have school the next day. Every fall our school has teacher workshops for two days, which means the teachers have to go in to school but we don't. It's a sweet deal!

And yeah, it was my twin sister's birthday but not mine. As strange as it sounds, I had to wait one more day to turn eleven. Ellie is thirteen minutes older than me. She was born at 11:55 on the night of the eighth, but I waited until after midnight to join the world, which means that she's officially a full day older. And she loves to rub this fact in my face any chance she gets. She's constantly reminding me that she's the older one. It's kind of like someone shoving stinky socks under your nose all the time. It gets old. And annoying.

Until recently she used to always call me her "Little Bro," but she promised that she'd cut that out as part of her new outlook, a.k.a. "Ellie's New Year." Over the past few weeks leading up to Rosh Hashanah, the Jewish New Year, we had a bunch of discussions about getting rid of some of our bad habits. Ellie's big goal is to try to be nicer to me and stop calling me by a name that I can't stand. We'll see how long that lasts. And besides, I pointed out to her that according to the Jewish calendar we actually *do* share a birthday because a new day begins when the sun goes down, not at midnight. So, depending on how you look at it, I'm not always a day behind her. Of course, I prefer to look at it that way. Ellie? Not so much.

So far she's kept her promise about not calling me her "Little Bro," but that's not to say that she doesn't drive me nuts in other ways because, believe me, she does. Like the time she "borrowed" my souvenir deck of playing cards from our trip to the Grand Canyon. She returned the box but it wasn't until several weeks later when I was in the middle of doing a magic trick for a couple of friends that I realized that four cards were missing. Every time I tried to impress my friends with the ace of spades mysteriously appearing, I would get a six of diamonds or a four of clubs or some other non-ace-of-spades card. It was so frustrating!

To be honest, I kind of like it when she does stuff to bug me because it gives me an excuse to get her back, which I actually find rather entertaining. And while I did promise that I'd be nicer to her too, I didn't *exactly* promise that I'd stop all the pranks I pull on her. I can't help it—it's so much fun! And she's such an easy target that it's too hard to resist. Sometimes I can even play the same joke on her over and over and she just doesn't catch on. I know it's not nice, but I really am a good guy, I promise! And even though she says she hates it when I play jokes on her, I think she secretly likes the attention. Sisters...who can understand them?

"Where are they, where are they, where are they?" Ellie muttered again a little louder than before, still pacing back and forth, now reminding me of a lioness circling and protecting her young cubs.

"YaYa, chill out, will you? They're not even five minutes late," I said looking at the new watch that *Bubby* and *Zayde,* our grandparents from Florida, sent me for my birthday.

"Okay, first of all," she said stopping right in front of my face, "please do *not* call me YaYa in front of my friends. It sounds like such a baby name. It's embarrassing!"

Ellie and I have these funny family nicknames. I'm YoYo and she's YaYa. When I was a baby and first attempted to say my Hebrew name, which is Yoel, all I was able to pronounce was YoYo. Ellie's Hebrew name is Yael, and thanks to me and my babbling, her nickname became YaYa. We still use these names all the time at home but not in front of our friends if we can help it. They are kind of goofy, I guess. Around friends we go by Joel and Ellie.

She started padding along the floor again.

"Seriously," I said, a bit louder than I had intended, "be cool, Ellie. What's the big deal if they're a few minutes late?" I really didn't get why she was so upset about it. In our family, we like to point out that Ellie is pretty much always late for everything, except for when we were born. That really was about the only time she ever got anywhere earlier than me. Sure, one time last month she got to the bus stop before I did, but let's just say it hasn't become a regular thing for her.

"Chill out, they'll be here. It's not like *you're* never late for anything," I reminded her. "They'll get here when they get here."

"Sure, that's easy for you to say. It's not your party."

"Thank goodness!" I mumbled under my breath.

"Wait, what?" She stopped pacing to look at me. "What did you say?"

"Nothing."

"I thought you didn't want a party. You're not jealous, are you?"

"What, of a gaggle of pre-teen girls braiding each other's hair and listening to the same five awful Corey McDonald songs over and over? Um, no. By the way, have you ever noticed that that guy can't even sing on key? Or in tune? Or in a way that doesn't sound like a howling monkey being run over by a truck?"

"Stop saying mean things about Corey!" my sister blurted out, defending her favorite singer as if he was her best friend. Or her boyfriend, which sometimes I think she might seriously believe. "He's amazing! You don't know what you're talking about. He's so talented! Not only can he sing, but he even wrote a measure or two of one of his own songs. And I heard that sometimes he writes some of his own lyrics. I'm pretty sure he wrote the whole chorus for the song 'Pretty, Like a Kitty' all by himself. I don't see *you* writing songs and lyrics. So stop picking on him!"

She was getting herself all worked up to the point that her ears turned a little bit pink. It's funny watching her get like that. I considered that if she kept it up she might get to the point of looking like she was wearing flaming red earmuffs. I love when that happens. I have to admit that sometimes I egg her on so I can watch her ears change from a light pink to a deep shade of crimson. It's fun to watch it happen in real-time. On the other hand, when I get super embarrassed, my entire face turns as red as a tomato and my freckles practically disappear. For Ellie, it's mostly the ears.

I looked at her with a blank stare. "'Pretty, Like a Kitty'? Is that for real? That's the genius of Corey McFlurry? I wrote better rhymes in kindergarten! Remember my epic poem about a balloon that was stolen by a baboon that he took into his rocket ship up to the moon? Now that's artistry."

She ignored me. "There's even a rumor going around that he might win a Grammy this year," she said triumphantly as if she just won her argument. Yep, the ears were now a little darker, the shade of a puppy's tongue. Then in a friendlier tone, "And as for my party, I have a weird feeling that you said you didn't want a big birthday bash, but you kind of do, don't you? Even though Mom and Dad are planning to take us all to Splash World to celebrate our birthdays as a family as soon as the holidays are over, I know that water parks are not really your idea of a good time. I get a sleepover *and* a trip to Splash World and you just get a day at the batting cages tomorrow. I don't get it. If you wanted to have a party, why didn't you just ask for one? It's not like they'd throw a party for my birthday and not for yours."

"YaYa—I mean—Ellie," I quickly corrected myself, "you need to get a grip on reality. Let's get a couple things straight. First of all, the day Corey McDonald wins a Grammy will be the day that Donald Duck takes over as principal of our school. And let's face it, that's not going to happen, and not only because he's a cartoon duck. I mean sure, that does present an obvious problem from the get-go, but even more than that the guy refuses to put on a pair of pants! And really, who ever heard of a principal who doesn't wear pants? There is a dress code, you know." I was pretty pleased with myself there. I really do crack myself up sometimes. (Or should I say "quack" myself up!) I shot Ellie back an identically triumphant smirk to match the one she flashed at me. I love being a smart aleck. And I love winning.

Ellie crossed her arms and rolled her eyes at me, looking up at the ceiling. I could practically see her impatience creeping up as if it had legs and was crawling up her body. But I wasn't done. "As for my birthday, I chose not to have a party because I hate big parties. You know that. I'm totally psyched to go to the batting cages with Ari and Micah in the morning. So, no, I'm not jealous. Not at all. Trust me."

Ellie eyed me suspiciously.

"And anyway, it's almost like I get an extra bonus birthday celebration since Ari is sleeping over tonight too," I reminded her.

"Yeah, and about that, you two'd better stay far away from us. No offense, but you guys are not invited to my sleepover," Ellie said. Did I sense a bit of fear in her voice? Rightfully so, because Ari and I had all sorts of pranks planned for the evening ahead.

"Don't worry," I replied, "you won't even know where we are." *Because we'll be hiding in your closet!* I thought with a delightfully mischievous chuckle. I can't help it. I don't play these tricks on anyone else. I mess around with my buddies and crack jokes all the time, and I've even earned the nickname "Jokin' Joel" at school. But there's nothing like pulling a prank on my sister. My older brother Jeremy, on the other hand, would probably pummel me to the ground if I tried anything on him so I pretty much stay out of his way. Jeremy is twelve and a half and in the seventh grade. He keeps to himself these days and I try to avoid him as much as possible because when he does talk to us he usually acts like a jerk. And it seems to be getting worse every day.

"What time is it?" Ellie asked, looking down at her bare wrist where her watch should have been. She also got one as a birthday gift from Bubby and Zayde.

"It's six thirty-nine," I said. "Where's your new watch?"

"Somewhere in my room," she answered distract-edly, still peering out the glass door. I usually refer to Ellie's bedroom as a black hole. I try not to lend her anything for fear of never seeing it again, like my deck of cards. She had one miraculous day a couple of weeks ago before Rosh Hashanah, when her room looked, well, almost as good as mine. It was neat and orga-nized, but that didn't last too long. I know she's mak-ing an effort but it really doesn't come that easily for her. I can't live like that. I need to know where every-thing is at all times. And if it can be alphabetized, numbered, and/or labeled, all the better.

At that moment a car pulled into the driveway. Ellie sprang to life as if she suddenly had hot coals in her underwear.

"Someone's here!" she squealed in a voice so high that my ears hurt. Had she brought her squeal up one more notch it would have been at a frequency that only dogs could hear, which at least, being out of my hearing range, wouldn't have been so painful for me.

...I can't speak for the dogs.

2

The Fun Begins

It was true, someone had arrived. But to Ellie's great disappointment it was the delivery guy from Niza's Pizzas.

"Mom, pizza's here," I yelled so she could hear me back in the kitchen. Mom had ordered a bunch of pizzas ahead of time for the party and planned to have them delivered just as the guests were arriving.

"Perfect! Right on time!" Mom sang out cheerfully as she rushed to the foyer with a checkbook in one hand and a pen in the other. As I went to the door to give her a hand with the boxes, I could've sworn I saw a shadowy figure pass by right behind the pizza dude as Mom paid him. It was getting pretty dark out and it was hard to see exactly what it was that walked by. It looked like it was some sort of an animal because I thought I spotted a long, thin tail. I didn't pay much attention since we have all sorts of wildlife living in our neighborhood. (And I'm not even referring to Jeremy and his seventh grade friends!) Not a day goes by that we don't see squirrels, chipmunks and rabbits racing across our front yard.

While we have a lot of animals living outside of our house, we don't have any living inside with us. Most of our friends have some sort of a pet, like a cat, a dog, or a hamster. A kid in my class even told us that he once had a pet porcupine. That doesn't seem like something I'd ever want to cuddle up with but to each his own, I guess. I'd always thought it would be cool to have a (normal) pet, like a dog or a cat, but I didn't think my parents would ever let us get one. My dad is always so busy working at his bookstore, The Silver Lining, and my mom's always doing a million things, including running her art business, helping Dad out in the store, and as she puts it, being the CEO of the Silver household.

I'd never gone so far as to actually ask my folks about getting a pet. I truly couldn't imagine that they'd ever say yes. Plus, I knew that if they did agree to adopt a pet they'd probably expect me to be the one to take care of it. My parents have never seemed to show much, if any, interest in animals. My brother would never pay attention because he's all caught up in his own self-involved teenage bubble. So, I bet I'd be the only one taking care of the little guy or gal. And who needs all that pressure? Of course my sister would offer to help, and I'm sure that she'd really mean to, but she's so disorganized, I'd worry that she'd forget to feed it or walk it. Or worse yet, I'd worry that she'd actually lose the poor thing altogether. If she brought a dog or a cat into her room, it could be days before we'd see it again!

I peered outside where I was trying to discover who or what it was trolling around out there. I turned away in time to see Ellie trudging back to the stairs where she plopped herself down, clearly disappointed that it was the pizza that had arrived rather than one of her friends. Mom rested the stack of square boxes on the hall table and turned to Ellie.

"No friends yet?" she said to my sister with a look more of pity than worry.

"Not yet," Ellie grumbled.

"Don't worry, honey, they'll show up soon. Maybe there was bad traffic or something."

Ellie sat and stared at the driveway, looking out the clear glass door, concentrating as if using a powerful gaze to make her friends magically materialize.

Out of nowhere, Jeremy appeared. It must have been his food radar going off because his arrival coincided exactly with the pizza delivery.

"We're having pizza tonight? Awesome!" he exclaimed. There isn't much that seems to get Jeremy excited these days but food is one of those rare exceptions. He "helped" Mom by carrying a pizza box into the kitchen and then walked back out to the foyer with a floppy slice hanging out of his mouth.

"Excellent 'za, Ma!" he said, chewing.

"Jay, how many years have you been living here?" Mom asked in her *this-isn't-really-a-question* tone of voice. "Please go eat that in the kitchen. You know I don't like you eating all around the house."

Jay is Jeremy's nickname. Ellie and I were about a year old when we became known as YaYa and YoYo. Jeremy, being a jealous three-year-old, wanted to be treated exactly like the two of us. That meant that he wanted a nickname based on his Hebrew name too. Problem is, his name is *Yeremiyahu*. He insisted that everyone call him YerYer but my parents refused because they said that it was a ridiculous name. (But YoYo isn't?) In the end, Ellie and I now have these sort-of secret nicknames that we only use at home, while Jeremy has all of his friends calling him Jay. He started junior high school last month and decided it was time to have a cooler name than Jeremy. I don't know how or why he decided that Jeremy isn't a cool name, but whatever. Older brothers...who can understand them? By the time Mom finished her sentence about Jeremy eating in the kitchen he was already done with the slice of pizza.

"What are you talking about, Mom?" he said making an outrageously fake innocent face, holding out his grease-covered hands. "What pizza?" Meanwhile, Dad walked by with a piece of pizza on a plate and a can of soda in his hand, heading into the office right off the foyer.

"MARK!" Mom yelled and pointed into the kitchen as if sending a naughty dog out to the doghouse. Dad jokingly tiptoed back into the kitchen.

"Busted!" Jeremy sang out following Dad, undoubtedly to get another slice (or four) for himself.

Suddenly we saw headlights as another car pulled up. Just like before, Ellie jumped up and ran to the door. This time it was my best friend, Ari Wolff. When the door opened I heard what sounded like a little "yip", and this time I definitely saw an animal's shadow out there. I couldn't tell what it was or how big it was, but it didn't matter. My best friend had arrived and so that meant that our fun was about to begin. Ari came into the house with a sleeping bag and pillow under one arm and a small, blue duffel bag in his other hand. Ellie plunked back down on the steps looking miserable.

"Hi, Mrs. Silver," Ari said to Mom.

"For the two thousandth time, Ari, please call me Debbie," Mom said. "Mrs. Silver is Mark's mom."

"Okay...well, uh, thanks for having me over," he stammered, clearly avoiding calling my mom by her first name. Ari's parents are very strict and proper and he was always taught to speak politely to grown-ups. Our family is way too laid back for that. I think maybe that's why Ari likes coming to our house so much. His house is like a museum with a million breakable things in the living room. There are three rooms we aren't even allowed to go into, and to tell you the truth, I'd be too afraid to take a single step into any of them anyway. I don't even want to think about what would happen if we broke something. We end up hanging out here a lot more often. It's much more comfortable for all of us.

I took Ari's duffel bag and led him upstairs toward my room. "Did you bring the fake mouse?" I asked in a whisper on the steps. Ari nodded.

When we reached the top of the staircase, we heard screams that sounded like a room full of screeching owls. Ari and I looked at each other, surprised that anyone could have heard us talking. But when we turned around we realized what was going on. The first two of Ellie's friends had arrived simultaneously and the three girls were jumping up and down and hugging in the entryway as if they hadn't seen each other in months. We both shook our heads, and without saying a word knew that we were thinking the same thing: *Girls are so weird!*

I gave Ari a thumbs-up sign as if to say, "We're safe." *And so the fun begins*, I thought as the two of us rushed off to my bedroom, escaping the squawking girls below.

3

Pizza in the Hut

After throwing Ari's stuff into my room, we ran down to the kitchen, inhaled several pieces of pizza then ventured to the basement to play foosball. Jeremy was chilling out in front of the TV and by this time Ellie was upstairs with all of her freaky friends. After gripping and twisting the foosball handles for about a hundred rounds, our hands were raw and practically bleeding. We had to stop playing before our hands fell off so we moved on to Phase Two of our evening's activities: back to my room to start planning our pranks.

It was really warm so I opened the window, which overlooks the backyard. All of a sudden, the patio lights flicked on outside and it was as if a light bulb flicked on in my head at the exact same time.

"Ari, quick, turn out the bedroom lights," I whispered. He did. Enough light seeped into my room from the hall and patio lights that Ari was able to see me motion for him to come and sit by the window. From there, we had a perfect view of Ellie and her crew coming out of the house and onto the patio with the rest of the pizza boxes and some drinks.

We hunched down under the window sill. I heard a bunch of those little yips again. It sounded like a very small animal. I closed my eyes and tried to picture what might make a noise like that. I really couldn't tell.

"Did you hear that?" I whispered to Ari.

"What? That little animal noise?" he asked.

"Yeah, what do you think it might be? I heard it earlier when I was waiting for you."

"No idea. Maybe it's a tiny bird or a chipmunk? It sounds pretty small."

"I don't know either. It doesn't sound like any animal I've ever heard out there before," I said. "Maybe we can check it out and see if we can solve the mystery."

"Okay, maybe later when we're done spying on the girls," Ari agreed. I like that we're often on the same page about what to do. That's why he's my best friend.

The girls started talking below us and we quickly forgot about the mysterious animal as we listened in on their conversation.

"Ellie, why is there a shack on your patio?" I heard one of her friends ask. This was perfect! We could hear everything!

"Oh, it's not really a shack," I heard Ellie say, "it's called a sukkah."

"A what-ah?" one girl asked.

"A sukkah. Come on, let's go inside it and I'll explain," Ellie said while leading them into the little hut-like structure. "We can eat the pizza in there."

Ari whispered to me, "They haven't eaten yet? What have they been doing all this time?"

"I'm guessing they were busy catching up. I mean, come on, they haven't seen each other since like, yesterday," I whispered back sarcastically. Ari chuckled.

We went back to peeking over the window sill. I could see Ellie, Megan (Ellie's best friend since kindergarten), Camille and the twins Sophie and Marissa (her friends from school), Mia, Jenna, Abby, and Dahlia (her

pals from Hebrew school) and some other girl that Ellie became friends with on her soccer team over the
summer. I always forget her name.

Sophie and Marissa Klein are identical twins and I
can never tell them apart. Sometimes I even refer to
them as "Sophissa" or "Marophie," because they seem
so interchangeable. Oh man, I can only imagine the
pranks I'd play if I had an identical twin! We'd switch
places and fool our teachers. We'd confuse our friends
by appearing and disappearing in different places. It
would be so much fun! Unfortunately, that's one trick I
could never pull off. Ellie may be my twin but she and I
are definitely not identical. Aside from the obvious fact
that I'm a boy and she's a girl, she has long, light
brown hair with some blond in it, and I have short,
dark hair and freckles. Plus, Ellie likes to show off that
she's about an inch taller than me—another thing she
does to bug me. In any case, nobody will ever get the
two of us mixed up.

"Okay, so, here we are in the sukkah," Ellie began,
sounding like a museum tour guide. "We build one of
these in our backyard every year for the Jewish holiday
of Sukkot. Actually, my mom and Joel build it and we
all decorate it."

"Your mom built this?" I heard a surprised voice
from down below.

"Yeah, she studied architecture in college before
she became an artist, so she's really into designing
stuff. And Joel's into using tools so they make a good
team." I appreciated getting some credit. And it wasn't
like she knew I was listening.

Ari turned to me. "Nice job with the sukkah. Next
year, call me and I'll help you with it. I'd love to build it

with you guys," he said, his voice increasing in volume to match his enthusiasm.

"Shhhh!" I shushed him, pointing at the open window, reminding him not to blow our cover. I purposely avoided answering his request, figuring I could deal later with whether or not to invite him next year. The truth is, I wasn't sure how to respond. I mean, Ari's my best friend and all, but I also look forward to putting up the sukkah with just my mom every year. It's our own special time.

I love that she's into building stuff, not just my dad. If it's a birdhouse you need, Dad's the guy for the job but when it comes to bigger projects he generally doesn't have the patience. He even said that if he built the sukkah, it would probably blow over like the straw house in the story of the Three Little Pigs. Mom's sukkah is much more Big-Bad-Wolf-proof. I guess I take after her in that way. Not to brag or anything, but since I'm really good at math and science, I recommended that we make the sukkah bigger next year because we always have so many guests, and I have some ideas on how to design it. I think it's so cool that we have a holiday on the Jewish calendar that involves construction!

Before I could even answer Ari about helping us build the sukkah next year, we heard the girls again. We had to be quiet in order to continue our mission of Operation Sukkah Sleepover.

"I'm Jewish but I don't know much about this holiday," one of Ellie's friends said. Depending on where they were standing, I could see some of the girls between the spaces of the beams on top of the sukkah where the roof will go, but I couldn't see who was speaking because the solid wood walls blocked my view.

"Yeah, it's not one of the more well-known holidays like Passover or Hanukkah, but it's definitely a big one. Sukkot happens to be one of our most awesome holidays. Isn't this so cool?" Ellie asked. I could see her looking around the sukkah with an air of pride, almost as if she came up with the whole idea of Sukkot on her own.

I was able to see Sophie (or Marissa) leaning back against the wall of the sukkah that was facing us.

"Careful! Don't lean on the walls, they're not that sturdy," Ellie said while pointing at the wooden panels. I was deeply offended by this. We did a masterful job of building that structure! I wanted to yell down to her, *"Yes they are! They could practically withstand a tornado!"* But obviously I couldn't do that since we were undercover. Plus, that may have been a bit of an over-exaggeration.

"And if you think these walls are flimsy," she continued while I huffed and crossed my arms in front of my chest, "you should see the ones made out of canvas. People use lots of different materials for the walls. In our family we kind of figured the sturdier the better, so ours are made of wood planks."

We?! When Mom and I bought the materials and built the sukkah, Ellie was nowhere to be found. She was probably in her room reading a book or playing a board game or something. I don't know exactly, but I can guarantee you that she wasn't part of the planning committee!

She continued. "And check it out, the sukkah doesn't even have a real floor or roof. The 'floor' is the ground," she said pointing down and then directing their attention upward, "and the roof, which we're going to finish putting up on Sunday, will be made of cornstalks. Some people use tree branches. The most important thing about the roof is that it has to be all natural. In Hebrew it's called 's'chach.' We usually put our s'chach up at the last minute, just before the holiday begins."

I could hear some of the girls trying to say the word s'chach. They sounded like a gang of cats coughing up hairballs.

"So, when you say the roof has to be all natural, does that mean it can be anything at all that's found in nature?" Dahlia asked looking up at the space that would eventually be a roof. I didn't understand why she was asking since she goes to Hebrew school with us but it didn't seem to faze Ellie. She simply kept on answering questions, apparently enjoying the role of resident Sukkot expert.

"Um," Ellie paused, "well, it has to be something that was once living."

"So, like, you could line the roof with *anything* that was once living and is all natural?" Dahlia summed up. I could hear a mischievous tone in her voice. I know that tone well from personal experience! She was definitely working her way up to some sort of a punch line. I couldn't wait to hear where she was going with this.

"Yeah, I guess so," Ellie replied.

"Could you use stuff like tropical palm branches?" Megan asked.

"Yup," Ellie responded.

"Wood?" Camille asked.

"Wood's good," Ellie said, "as long as it hasn't been made into anything like furniture. So you can't put wooden chairs up there and call it a roof," she finished with a giggle.

Dahlia deadpanned, "How about a big bearskin rug? Or maybe rotten banana peels? Those are all natural. Ooh, what about dead squirrels? Maybe you could take some clothespins and hang them by their tails from the beams on top."

Oh, I liked that one! That's totally something I would have said.

"Eeew!" nine voices screeched together. Dahlia clearly enjoyed grossing them out.

"What? No! Who would want dead squirrels hanging over their heads?" Ellie yelped sounding like she was going to gag.

"What is wrong with you?" Marophie asked Dahlia, looking disgusted.

"Nothing! Oh my gosh! You guys, I was kidding! Can't you take a joke?" Ari and I snickered. Oh yeah, I could definitely overlook the fact that she's a girl, and could see myself hanging out with her. I totally got her sense of humor.

"So, aside from that just being grosser than gross," Mia said, "the s'chach has to be *plant* material of some sort that's no longer living, so no bears or squirrels. And rotten banana peels? Well, they're plant material, but really? That's disgusting. They would stink!" The girls laughed. "And you can't put your sukkah under a tree and use the branches as the s'chach. They have to be detached from the tree."

I nodded approvingly at Ari. I was very surprised at how much I was enjoying the girls' discussion. Usually I liked spying on them purely to get a good laugh. But this was turning out to be very eye-opening. And Mia is one of Ellie's few friends that I can actually tolerate. She's one of the smart kids in our class but she's not an obnoxious know-it-all like this other girl in our class named Hannah Glick. That girl drives me crazy.

"I think it's so cool that you have a sukkah of your own," Abby said changing the subject from dead animals. "My parents don't build one. The only one I ever go to is the one we visit at synagogue with Rabbi Green during Hebrew school."

"Well, we certainly don't have one," said Jenna. "There's not much room in our apartment for a sukkah! I guess maybe we could make a small one on our terrace."

"Doesn't your terrace have another one right above it?" Mia asked.

"Yeah," Jenna answered, "the Frank family lives above us."

"Then it wouldn't work. Don't you remember? Part of the deal with the sukkah is that if you're sitting inside you have to be able to look up through the roof and see the sky and the stars. You can't have anything on top of it, so it really wouldn't work at your place," Mia explained.

"Sad! I forgot about that," Jenna said.

"Impressive," I whispered to Ari. Mia clearly knew what she was talking about.

"When my family visited Israel over the summer," Mia continued, "we noticed that some of the apartment buildings were built in such a way that the terraces were staggered so they had nothing above them. The people who lived there could actually build a sukkah right on their terrace, and when they sat in it, they could look up and see the stars with nothing blocking their view of the sky."

"That's so cool," Jenna said.

"And very smart," added Ellie.

"Like, I still don't get it, guys," Soccer Girl said, "this whole thing is very confusing."

"Oh sorry, Claire," Ellie said. I made a mental note to try to remember that Soccer Girl's name was Claire. "Let me start over again."

"No, no, no, no!" they all shouted at once. "Please don't start over again!"

"I mean, like, didn't you just have a holiday? Isn't that why you've been out of school so much lately?" Camille asked.

"Yeah, well, actually we had two holidays so far. First we celebrated Rosh Hashanah." She turned to Megan. "That was when you invited me to go to Splash World with your family but I couldn't go."

"Yeah, sure, Rosh Hashanah, that was just like, last week," Megan said.

Claire said, "I've heard of that one."

Ellie continued. "Then yesterday we finished Yom Kippur. That's the really serious day when we fast. No eating or drinking. Nada, nothing."

"Hey, you didn't call me this year when it was over to complain about how hungry you were all day," Megan replied with a chuckle.

"You're right. I was too excited and busy getting ready for my birthday! Anyway, the next holiday up is Sukkot, which begins on Sunday night. This one always seems to sneak up on us right after Yom Kippur."

"So, I guess that explains the little booth thinga-mabob that shows up magically on my neighbors' driveway every year. My brother and I thought it was like a spooky pre-Halloween thing that would mysteriously appear and disappear! We thought it was like a ghost shack or something," said Camille. The girls all laughed.

"Nope, nothing spooky or mysterious. Sukkot is a really happy, fun holiday that celebrates the fall harvest," Ellie explained.

"So, why do you have so many holidays?" Claire asked, taking a sip of her drink.

"Well, at this time of the year it does seem like every other day it's another holiday, and believe it or not, when this one's over, we have one more set of holidays called *Shmini Atzeret* and *Simchat Torah*. Then we're done until Hanukkah," Ellie answered.

"Yeah, Hanukkah, that's like Christmas, right?" Claire asked.

"Um, no. It happens around the same time as Christmas, but it's a completely different holiday," Ellie said much more patiently than I would have answered. She really seemed to be enjoying fielding all these questions.

"Before you get into Hanukkah, tell us already, what's the deal with the hut?" Camille questioned.

"I know I told you already that the name of the holiday is Sukkot. That's the plural of sukkah, which is what this 'hut' is."

"Um, yeah, so, like, what do you do with it?" Claire asked.

"First, we build it. Next we decorate it and cover the roof with the s'chach, and then we eat our meals in it."

"How long do you keep it up here?" someone asked.

"Well, the holiday only lasts for one week but sometimes it takes us a long time to take it down. We're pretty quick to build it but not always so quick about putting it away."

"That's how we are with our Christmas lights. One year we had them up on our house until Easter!" Megan said. "I can't believe that after being your friend since even before kindergarten, I've never been inside this thing. So, that's it? You guys build it and eat in it?"

"Well, sometimes we sleep in here with our dad," Ellie said.

"I never heard of that custom!" Abby said.

"Why just with your dad?" Camille asked.

"It's just a Silver family tradition. We tend to have a lot of those. Mom has a weird thing about sleeping in the sukkah. I think she may have had a bad experience once," Ellie said.

"What kind of bad experience?" Sophissa asked.

"I'm not really sure. I think it had something to do with a raccoon, though," Ellie answered vaguely.

"Hey, I have an idea!" Jenna said. "Since we're already eating out here, how about if we sleep out here tonight too? It's a warm night. It would be almost like a camping trip."

"But with indoor plumbing!" Claire chimed in.

Ari and I looked at each other with knowing looks. This was getting better and better by the minute!

"It's okay with me, if you all want to. I'll have to ask my parents, but if they say it's all right, I say let's do it. Does everyone want to sleep outside?" Ellie asked.

"I do!" "Yeah!" "Cool!" came a chorus of girls' voices. They were all pretty psyched, although I noticed that Marissa (or maybe it was Sophie—I wish I could tell them apart!) was very quiet and didn't join in with the cheers and whoops. She just kind of stood back, biting her fingernails, looking nervously around at the sukkah.

"What's the deal with the raccoon?" Marissa (or Sophie) asked. "Do you get raccoons in here?"

"I have never seen a raccoon in here. Not ever," Ellie responded. "There's nothing to worry about. Whatever happened was a long time ago and not at this house." She jumped up and cheered, "So, is this is going to be the best birthday party ever or what?!"

"Yeah it is!" I whispered to Ari.

"Too bad they don't know that there *is* something to worry about!" he added and put his hand up for a high five.

Ellie went back inside, undoubtedly to ask permission to sleep in the sukkah. The rest of the girls followed her into the house one by one. It was time for us to get busy.

"Where should we begin?" I asked.

Ari opened his duffel bag with such a look of pride you'd think he had an Olympic gold medal in there. We started rummaging through his stuff until we found exactly what we were looking for.

4

Shack Attack

Apparently our parents gave them permission because within twenty minutes, the girls were all set up outside in our roofless sukkah, and Ari and I were all set up in my room. We crouched down below my window, listening to the girls' ridiculous gabfest about whether or not they're allowed to wear makeup. (Ellie is not, in case you were wondering.) So much for the interesting discussion they were having earlier. Ari and I rolled our eyes at each other. How is it that some girls can spend so much time talking about all that junk? Girls...who can understand them?

In the tradition of great pranksters, Ari had brought a massive amount of balloons, which we proceeded to fill with water. I jiggled a red one around in my hand. What a great invention. The person who came up with this idea was an absolute genius. Water balloons: now *that's* something I *can* understand!

"Looks like 'rain'," Ari said quietly, making air quotes.

"Yeah, with an excellent chance of 'heavy precipitation'," I agreed with air quotes of my own, speaking in a hushed weather-announcer voice.

I removed the window screen and we collected all of our water balloons, hugging them close to us, getting ready to hammer the unsuspecting girls below. It was really great that the sukkah wasn't all done yet.

Since we still hadn't put up the s'chach, with just enough aim we could get the water balloons right into the sukkah and nail the girls. If we missed, they'd hit the beams or the tops of the walls and break and splatter there. Either way, it was a terrific plan.

Ari looked at me and said, "Let's do a trial run and throw one balloon before we really let 'em have it. It'll just confuse them a bit."

I nodded. "Do you want to go first or should I?" I asked.

"Go ahead, it's almost your birthday, you can have the honor," Ari said.

I quietly calculated in my head how much force I would need to exert to get enough lift in the air so the balloon would have the right amount of arc to successfully soak the girls. (Math and science again—they always come in handy.) Once I was ready, I held the balloon out the window and whispered, "Bombs away!"

Much to my surprise, my calculations must have been off because the balloon didn't quite make it into the sukkah. It merely landed with a quiet, dull "plunk" on the grass. As far as I could tell, it didn't even break. The girls were still cackling and giggling as they launched into a meaningful debate about nail polish colors.

"Try again," Ari suggested.

I took a green balloon this time and felt the water slosh around inside of it. It was a bit fuller and felt slightly heavier in my hand, so I figured that this one would be more successful, given the new variable to my equation.

"Take two," I whispered.

I held my hand out the window, and this time tossed it with a little more force. I couldn't believe it! A strong breeze came right at that moment and made it veer off course. It blew in the opposite direction of the sukkah and landed across the yard. I couldn't even see if it broke or not.

"Oh, come on!" I muttered.

"Try again," Ari coaxed. "Third time's a charm."

Right then, Jeremy walked by my doorway. Uh oh! We had forgotten to close the door.

"Quick, hide the balloons!" I whisper-barked at Ari.

"What's up mini dudes?" Jeremy asked as he let himself into my room. I can't even imagine what he'd do if I just strolled uninvited into his room. He'd absolutely go berserk.

"Nothing much," I answered casually, while turning to face him and simultaneously hiding a handful of balloons behind my back in the dark.

"Whatcha hiding?" He stepped closer to me.

"Nothing—at least nothing that's any of your business. Ari and I are just doing some stuff that doesn't concern you," I said with unexpected bravery. It's not that I'm scared of Jeremy (well, maybe I am a little), it's just that he's almost a full head taller than me. He had a major growth spurt while he was at sleep-away camp this summer. When he got on the bus in June to go to Camp Kingman, I was right about up to his chin. When he got off the bus in August, he was almost as tall as our mom. Now I'm only up to his shoulder. It's like someone cemented his feet to the ground, hooked him up to a crane by his armpits and stretched him out. Maybe the camp food isn't as bad as everyone says it is. Anyway, had I been the least bit smart I wouldn't have started up with Jeremy, but clearly I wasn't being all that sharp.

"Really, let me see what 'nothing' looks like," Jeremy said as he flicked on the light and lunged toward me. Ari, thinking fast, quickly closed my shades. I tried to back up, but bumped into the window sill. Before I knew it, I was wet. Water soaked the small of my back, ran down my legs and onto the floor. Ari, being the good friend that he is did his best not to bust out laughing. He did a good job too—for a while—but then he cracked up, which made me crack up too. I looked so ridiculous standing there with a wet bottom half, looking like I had an accident in my pants. My face felt hot, and I could just imagine how red it must have turned. Probably as red as that first balloon I held in my hand.

"WATER BALLOONS?" Jeremy exclaimed, "EXCELLENT!"

"SHHHHHHH!" I loudly shushed him, waving my arms around to get him to be quiet. I dove at the window to shut it from behind the closed shades.

Jeremy walked past me to the window, pulled the window shade back and peered out. He looked at the girls in the unfinished sukkah then looked at me with a smug, obnoxious smirk. I did not like where this was going.

"Okay, here's the deal," he said flipping his baseball cap so that the brim was facing backwards. He walked over to my desk, turned the chair around, threw one long leg over the bottom, straddled it, and sat down. Leaning over the back of the seat, using the most conceited, intimidating voice, he said, "I can either tell Mom about what you guys are doing up here and you'll be so grounded you probably won't be allowed out of the house until you graduate from college." He paused and lowered his voice in a conniving tone. "Or you can let me in on the action and I won't say a word. Your choice. What'll it be?"

I was more shocked than anything. Since when did Jeremy want to hang out with his "uncool" brother and his equally uncool best friend? When we were really young, Ellie and I totally looked up to Jeremy, even though he's not even two years older than us. But over the past couple of years and definitely since he came back from camp, he's been acting like he's way too mature to be bothered with us "little kids" and the little kid things we like to do. He's much too cool to be seen with us and definitely too absorbed in his own world to even talk to us unless he's teasing or making fun of us. Now the only "looking up" to him that I do is to see him. And from my vantage point, I can almost see straight up his nose. It's not a pretty sight.

I looked at Ari and shrugged my shoulders as if to say, "Do we really have a choice?" The look on Ari's face matched mine.

"Fine, you can join us, but we still haven't gotten the first shot. You need to wait your turn," I said faking a confident whisper.

"Okay Betsy Wetsy," he said in a mocking voice, pointing to my wet pants, "whatever you say."

It might be worth getting grounded until eternity just to not have to hang out with him, I thought for a moment. I don't think he could be any more unpleasant if he tried. I chose to not let him ruin Ari's and my good time.

"I'm going to change out of these clothes and then we'll get back to business," I said to Ari, purposely ignoring Jeremy, hoping that maybe he'd get the hint and leave. Unfortunately, he did not. I grabbed a change of clothes and went to the bathroom down the hall. There was no way I was going to change in front of my obnoxious brother. He'd undoubtedly find something to tease me about.

I went as fast as I could because I didn't want to leave Ari alone with Jeremy any longer than necessary. I got a terrible image in my head of my brother hanging Ari from the light fixture in my room. I imagined Ari with his legs and arms flailing, spinning around attached to the ceiling fan by his underwear in a wedgie. Just thinking of what Jeremy might do made me run down the hall even faster. To my great relief, the two of them were simply sitting there talking. I figured that their conversation was about camp, which is all Jeremy seems to want to talk about these days.

I entered my room and said in a very important-sounding voice, "Okay, men, let's get busy. We have some serious work to do here."

"Hold on," Ari said. "Jay and I were just talking and we have an even better idea. If we use water balloons, they'll have proof that we threw them, since there will be broken balloon pieces all over the ground. If we switch to squirt guns, the girls will get wet, but there won't be any hard evidence that we had anything to do with the sudden 'cloudburst'. It was Jay's idea and I think he's got a good point."

Jeremy shot me an arrogant look as if to say *I'm even better at your own game than you are.* I had to admit, it was good thinking—brilliant, actually. But I didn't want to let on that I was impressed with his scheming mind because for all I knew one of these days he might decide to turn it on me. Instead I casually replied with a slight shrug, "Uh, okay, we can try that, I guess. I'll go to the garage and find our Super Soakers."

Within a few minutes the three of us were hunched by my window with the shades up and the lights off, back to snooping on the girls. Each of us held a different, fully loaded squirter in our hands. We were ready for action. And this time, we remembered to close the door.

5

Raindrops Keep Falling on My Head

Bull's-eye!" I exclaimed quietly as my stream of water hit the top of the sukkah. The three of us hid under the window sill enjoying the thrill of victory.

"Yes!" Ari said as he high-fived me.

"Nice shot," Jeremy admitted.

We peered over the sill to view the damage. As expected, the girls didn't know what was going on. I saw Marissa (or Sophie) look up expectantly at the sky. Then I heard her say, "You guys, is it supposed to rain tonight?"

"Nah, look at the sky. It's a perfectly clear night. Not a cloud in sight," Megan said.

"I thought I felt a rain drop," Marissa (or Sophie) said.

How did they not *all* feel it? I wondered. Must have hit something else in the sukkah, I guess. Time for another small squirt and then the full-on downpour would begin.

Ari took his turn. "Look out below!" he whispered and squeezed his trigger a couple of times.

Another successful shot.

"You can NOT tell me that you didn't feel that one!" I heard one of them say in a high-pitched, whiny voice.

"I felt that," Megan said.

"Yeah, me too," said Ellie.

"You know what's funny?" Mia asked (at least I think it was Mia; it was hard to see but it sounded like her voice). "At the end of Sukkot we start to pray for rain. Or at least we're praying for rain in Israel. It's the beginning of the rainy season there and since it's so dry the rest of the year, we pray that they'll get enough water to keep them going through the year. Meanwhile, we hope that it *won't* rain here while we're sleeping and eating in the sukkah! I really, really hope it doesn't rain tonight."

"Same here," Ellie agreed sulkily. "It would ruin all of our plans."

The girls started yammering about the weather, which of course led to another brilliant dialogue about how rain makes some of their hair frizzy or ruins their hairstyles after they've spent almost an hour making them perfect. Ari and I shook our heads in disbelief and once again rolled our eyes at each other. We waited a few minutes for them to calm down and not suspect anything. Then each of us took our squirters in two hands to steady ourselves.

"Let's see how quickly their hair frizzes up," Ari said.

"On the count of three, let 'er rip," I commanded like an army general. "One, two... threeeeeee!"

Our "storm" began. The water splattered all over the girls. This time there was no mistaking that they all got wet.

"What the...?" "Huh?" "Oh, shoot, I guess it *is* raining!" "We'd better make a run for it!" They jabbered all at once while we three kept squirting. They collected their sleeping bags and stuff and scrambled into the house.

"Oh my goodness!" Ari panted in fits of laughter. With his finger still on the trigger and the water gun resting on his stomach, he rolled onto his back on the floor, laughing hysterically and trying to catch his breath. He looked like a ladybug flipped over on its shell. "This is too good!"

"Yeah, we sure got 'em!" I agreed.

"Now what?" Jeremy asked. "They went inside, so how are we going to keep bugging them?"

"First of all," I looked up at him, "*we* aren't going to keep bugging them—at least not a 'we' that includes you. You got to do the water raid with us. Now you get to leave us alone."

Ari flashed me a look that said, "Oh no. Don't go there. Not good...."

But it was too late. I said it and I managed to make Jeremy mad. Really, really mad. German-Shepherd-foaming-at-the-mouth-after-you've-taken-away-his-chew-toy mad.

He didn't say anything, though. Instead, he calmly turned and started for the door. I looked at Ari and we both collapsed on my bed feeling relieved. That was until...

"MOM!" Jeremy bellowed as he headed down the hall toward the stairs.

"We have to stop him!" I yelled to Ari while pulling his sleeve to get him up off the bed. "If my mom finds out that we were spraying the girls, I'm going to be in so much trouble. And for sure we can kiss our day at the batting cages tomorrow goodbye."

The two of us raced down the hall and tackled Jeremy. He went down with a huge thud, his leg banging into the wall really hard. One of the pictures of Mom's great-grandma Miriam fell down and almost hit us. Fortunately it landed so that it was just leaning against the wall. We were lucky that the glass in the frame didn't break. But it was enough of a commotion to send my mom running to the foot of the stairway. We couldn't see her from around the corner. More importantly, she couldn't see us.

"Boys?" She questioned in a concerned tone from down below. "What's going on?"

Ari covered Jeremy's mouth while I pinned his arms down, lying on top of his wriggling, much-larger-than-me body.

"Nothing, Mom!" I called back. "Just goofing around with Jay." I figured Mom would like the idea of us including Jeremy in our fun.

"Oh, okay. But cut out the rough-housing inside, boys," Mom replied. "I don't want you to break anything. No wild games, please."

"Okay, we'll stop," I answered, trying to sound natural while wrestling with Godzilla. Jeremy mustered up his strength and rolled himself on top of me, pinning my arms down to the floor.

"Who's the boss now, loser?" he practically spat at me.

"You can't...tell Mom...what we were...doing!" I gasped, trying to breathe with Jeremy on top of me after I heard Mom walk away from the bottom of the stairs.

"Why not, Monkey Brains?" Jeremy retorted.

"Because if you do you'll get us all in trouble since you were doing it too."

Jeremy was now sitting on my chest. I felt like I was being crushed under a fallen building. I had to get out of there and I knew I couldn't win this wrestling match by physical strength since Jeremy was so much bigger than me. I had to beat him the only way I could. I had to play dirty. "Plus," I added, "I'll be sure to let Ilana Goldsmith, and everyone else for that matter, know that you definitely have a crush on her." (Yuck! Twelve-and-a-half-year-old boys with crushes…really, who can understand them?)

"You wouldn't," he growled, easing up on my arms. You see, even big, bully, older brothers have a weak spot. And it's always good to know what that weak spot is just in case you ever need it.

"Oh, I would. All it would take is one phone call to Zachary. He would love to get some dirt on his older sister."

"You're *so* gonna get it," Jeremy said with clenched teeth.

Ari the peacemaker said, "Hey, Jeremy, how about if we drop this whole thing and you hang with us some more. It was fun bugging the girls with you and we've only just started our evening activities. We have lots more stuff planned. Why don't you join us?"

I looked at Ari with a mixture of confusion, anger, and betrayal. How could he invite Bigfoot to join us? Didn't he know that he was about to destroy our whole evening?

Ari winked at me to let me know that he had a plan. Ari always has a plan. He's like the smartest kid in the fifth grade. Well, actually, we both are. In fact, we often compete against each other to see who gets better grades on our tests. But when it comes to "street smarts," Ari wins hands down. He's always ready with a quick comeback or an excellent game plan, which is what I guess he was up to now.

"Nah," Jeremy grunted as he climbed off of me, "I don't need to hang out with little, baby fifth-graders." Then he pointed at me, his finger practically squishing my nose. "You mention anything about Ilana and you're dead meat.... Not that I really like her...'cause I don't. She's okay and all...but I don't...." His voice trailed off and he got this weird look on his face. He stood up and started walking away, lumbering down the hall like a real tough guy.

I shot Ari a look from behind my brother's back and silently mouthed to him, "Oh, he SO likes her!" Ari read my lips and nodded in agreement, confirming my assessment. Like I said, it's always good to have some ammunition in case you ever need it.

"Are you sure you don't want to join us, Jay?" Ari called to his back. "We have lots of other cool things to do." He was really piling it on now.

Jeremy didn't even have the courtesy to respond. He merely sauntered into his room, slammed the door, and blasted his music, making the walls vibrate. It caused enough of a tremor for Great-Great-Grandma Miriam's picture to topple over face down on the carpet. As I picked up the nail that had fallen out of the wall, stuck it back in the hole with my thumb and re-hung the frame, I turned to Ari and said, "Nice work, Mr. Slick! Way to get him out of our hair."

"Thanks. Now, where were we?"

We raced back to my room, closed the door, and dug into Ari's bag of tricks.

"What should we do next?" I asked.

Ari rifled through the duffle bag. "Aha!" he said pulling out a digital camera and a mini voice recorder. We were back in business.

6

Spy Guys

The girls finally realized that the threat of rain was over and went back outside with their sleeping bags, pillows, and other assorted girl-stuff. Ari and I played "Spy Guys" for a while, snapping secret pictures of the girls with Ari's camera, which had a super-strong zoom lens, and trying to listen in to what they were chattering about. After a while, we got bored listening to them go on and on about Corey McDonald and how "cute" he is. Ugh. And really, how many pictures of them doing their nails could we take? We decided to head downstairs to watch a movie.

On our way to the basement we passed our home office on the main floor. We saw Jeremy sitting in front of the computer, nodding his head in time, we assumed, with the music coming out of the earphones he had on. We weren't able to hear the music so it was pretty funny to see him sitting there looking like a human bobble-head. The Spy Guys were on the case. We couldn't help but wonder what he was up to. We ever so quietly crawled into the room on all fours like sneaky cats, trying to see what he was doing. It was very helpful that he had the music blaring into his ears.

It looked like he was using the Instant Messenger function and chatting online with someone while simultaneously playing a video game. I squinted but couldn't see well enough so I motioned to Ari to retreat with me from the room.

Once in the hall, I said to Ari, "Agent Rooster Neck, wait here, I have an idea."

Ari saluted me and said, "Roger that Agent Freckle Face."

I sprinted up the steps to my room and headed straight to my closet. I pulled out the big box of science gear that I had organized with items beginning with the letters "A" through "F". Stored neatly among the batteries, beakers, bulbs, other assorted "B" items were the binoculars that my Aunt Rachel got for me a couple of years ago when I was really into bird watching. Then I went to my desk drawer and pulled out a small pad of paper. I also took a sharpened pencil from the cup on top of my desk.

I hustled out of my room and got as far as the top of the staircase when I suddenly thought of something else. I turned right around and headed back to my closet. This time I opened up the box with my "W" supplies and grabbed two walkie-talkies. I then ran down the steps with the strap of the binoculars swinging back and forth around my neck and one walkie-talkie in each back pocket. I placed the talkies on the hall table and tiptoed toward the office. When Ari saw me, he nodded and gave me a big thumbs-up, letting me know that he totally understood what I was up to. It's pretty cool. I have this sort of connection with two people in the world: my twin sister and my best friend. We are so very much on the same wavelength that I can practically communicate with each of them without ever saying a word.

We snuck back inside the office, crawling on our elbows commando style. I held the binoculars up to my eyes. I almost burst out laughing, but cupped my hand over my mouth and managed to control myself. Ari was dying to know what was going on and motioned for me to pass the binoculars over to him. I quietly slid the strap off my neck and passed them to him. He shrugged and made a face at me to indicate that he didn't understand what was going on. He passed them back to me.

I looked at the screen and jotted down what I saw:

J: Sup?

I: NM. Sup w/u?

J: U do ur hw 4 himmel?

I: No u?

J: Not yet

I: U goin 2 Leah's bm?

J: Yeah. U?

I: yep

J: cool.

I: BTW what r u doing 2m?

J: IDK. U?

I: NM. Want 2 hang?

J: K

I: cool it'll B fun

J: IKR

I: Ya

J: Don't 4get 2 bring the monkey hat

I: ROTFL! UR2F!!!

J: LOL!

Then Jeremy wrote: BRB. Luckily, he didn't get up right away. I grabbed Ari's shirt and pulled him out of there so fast that I almost ripped his sleeve right off.

When we were a safe distance from the office, Ari asked, "What the heck? Why'd you yank me out of there like that? And what was he typing? I couldn't understand it!"

"Sorry I had to pull you out so quickly," I explained, "but Jeremy was cyber-flirting with that girl Ilana that he claims he doesn't like. And when he wrote BRB that meant 'be right back' so I thought he was going to get up. I didn't want him to see us."

"Ah," he said. Then he looked at me with a wrinkled nose. "Cyber-flirting?" he said, looking like he was going to be sick.

"Yeah, this is juicy!" I said. "They were IM'ing. It's like texting. Teenagers are really into it. Jeremy's been doing it for a while already."

"I know all about texting, but I couldn't understand it. Could you?" Ari asked.

I looked down at my notes. "Yeah, I got it all. Here's what it said pretty much word for word. Jeremy started by saying 'what's up?' and she answered, 'not much, what's with you?' He then asked if she did her homework for Mr. Himmel's class yet and she said she didn't and asked if he did, which he did not. Then she asked him if he was going to Leah's bat mitzvah and he said yes. She said she was going too. He said, 'cool'."

Ari made a face and shook his head. I continued. "Then she asked, 'By the way, what are you doing tomorrow?' and he answered, 'I don't know, how about you?' She said, 'Not much, want to hang out?' He said 'okay' and she replied, 'Cool, it'll be fun.' He said, 'I know, right?' And she said 'yeah.' Then he said 'Don't forget to bring the monkey hat'—I have no idea what that is—but apparently she did because she said she was 'rolling on the floor laughing' and told him that he's too funny. He said LOL, which means that he was laughing out loud."

"Well, I know that," Ari said. "But he wasn't really laughing out loud."

"Yeah, but I'm guessing she wasn't actually rolling on the floor laughing, either. They're just expressions," I added. "Anyway, the last thing he wrote was BRB, which is when I grabbed you."

"How do you know all this?" Ari asked.

"What? You think I only spy when you're around?"

"Hey, I have an idea!" Ari said. "How about if we use my cell phone to call Jeremy?"

"Hang on one sec," I said. "How can you have a cell phone and not know how to text?"

"I only got it because my parents wanted to keep tabs on me. I really don't use it for anything other than calling my mom to let her know that I need to get picked up or whatever."

"Gotcha," I said.

"Anyway, we can pretend that it's Ilana once he's offline with her. He won't recognize the number and 'Ilana' could say that she's using her mom's phone. I can disguise my voice pretty well. He'll never know! Listen." He cleared his throat and in a high falsetto voice said, "Hi Jay. It's Ilana. Wanna be my boyfriend?" Then back in his regular voice he said, "How much would you love to get him back for all the pain and suffering he's caused you over the years?"

It did sound tempting. We could have a lot of fun with this.

"All right," I said, "but we have to be super careful that he doesn't figure out it's us. Let's go into the tool room in the basement and do it. He'd never think to look for us in there." We tiptoed toward the stairs to go down.

"Hold up," I said to Ari. "I just want to run upstairs and get my slippers. The basement floor is kind of cold." I handed Ari one of the two walkie-talkies from the table. "Here, Agent Rooster Neck, take this down to the basement so we can communicate while I go upstairs."

"Roger that, Agent Freckle Face," Ari said. "I'll keep my eyes open for Bigfoot too." I guess Jeremy had an official code name now. Cool.

Once in my room, I passed my bulletin board and stopped abruptly before reaching the closet. Kind of like the way a car on a roller coaster comes to a sudden, jerky stop when it reaches the station, even though it barely has enough time to slow down before getting there. (I'm really not a big roller coaster fan but I do like learning about the physics involved in the rides. Ask me anything about g-forces, friction, mass, kinetic and potential energy, and I'm all over it. But don't try to get me to ride one of those things.)

Anyway, there was my conscience staring me in the face, making me feel guilty and rethink all that I had been planning to do. It was my conscience in the form of a photograph.

I pressed the button on my walkie-talkie, held it up to my mouth, and said, "Agent Rooster Neck, this is Agent Freckle Face, do you read me? Over."

A scratchy reply came from the little box in my hand, "I copy, Agent Freckle Face. Over."

"Agent Rooster Neck, abort Mission Bigfoot. I repeat, abort Mission Bigfoot."

There was no reply for a few seconds. Then my walkie-talkie came to life again, "Seriously?" So much for the spy-speak. However, I wasn't ready to be done.

"Agent Rooster Neck, do you read me?"

"Yeah, I'll be right there," Ari replied over the radio sounding extremely disappointed. Within seconds, he was standing with me in my bedroom.

"What happened?" he asked.

"I can't do it."

"You can't do what? Find your slippers?"

"No," I said apologetically, "I can't play the trick on Jeremy."

"What? Why not?" he cried out, looking like I had just ruined his life, as if I told him it was now illegal to eat candy.

"Last week, during Rosh Hashanah, Ellie and I had a serious talk about *t'shuvah*, you know, the Hebrew word for repentance."

"Yeah, I was there for that discussion at Hebrew school too, remember? So?"

"Well," I continued, "we also talked a lot about it at home and as a result we sort of started this new Silver family tradition. Ellie gave me a 'T'shuvah Shoebox'—"

"Hold on. A what?" Ari interrupted.

"A T'shuvah Shoebox. It's a shoebox and we each put something in it that represents what we'd like to do better this year—."

He interrupted me again, "Why a shoebox? I don't get it."

"It's a long story. I'm not going to get into it right now. Anyway, it's all about how we'd like to improve our behavior. Ellie gave me this picture." I pointed to the snapshot pinned to my bulletin board showing us at about eighteen months old, laughing hysterically in a kiddie pool. Ellie had written on the top corner in permanent marker, *YaYa and YoYo, BTFs. (Best Twins Forever.)* "She wanted to try to remember to be nicer to me and not call me names. She said the picture reminded her of how much fun we have together when we aren't driving each other crazy. I promised to try to be nicer to her as well. And that includes pulling pranks on her. And that translates to Jeremy too."

Ari looked disappointed. "Why'd you have to go and make a dumb promise like that?" he questioned, looking completely baffled. "This is what you do! You are 'Jokin' Joel' the prankster. Everyone knows that."

"Yeah, but I really do want to try to keep my promise. It's not easy but if I'm going to expect Ellie and Jeremy to be nicer to me, then I need to do the same for them."

"It doesn't seem like Jeremy's keeping up his end of the bargain. He's not exactly being nicer to you," Ari argued.

"Well, he only promised to be more patient and get less annoyed with us. He never actually said he'd actively be nicer. I think he was very careful with his words."

"So pounding you into the floor is okay?"

"Technically, no," I replied, "but just because he's being a jerk doesn't mean that I should be one too."

"So no more pranks on the girls or Jeremy? That was all we had planned for the whole evening! What do you want to do instead, T'shuvah Boy?" Ari asked, flopping onto on my bed looking bored.

"How about if we go watch a movie like we were going to before we got sidetracked with Jeremy and his cyber-flirting?" I suggested.

Once again we headed downstairs. We walked past the open door to the office and saw Jeremy now video chatting and laughing with Ilana. How could he deny that he liked her? It was so obvious! I was proud of myself for remembering and keeping up my end of the t'shuvah deal. As we passed by, Jeremy saw us, got up out of his chair and slammed the door in our faces to make it clear that we weren't welcome. He sure was making it hard to be nice to him.

I turned to Ari. "We'd better find a really good and long movie tonight. For his sake."

7

Shul School

The next day was Friday, my actual birthday. It's nice to be a twin, but I like that I also still get my own special day. Micah Salzman, another good friend of mine, came over in the morning and Ari, Micah, and I had a great time at the batting cages. We spent more than four hours hitting balls, eating treats, and playing in the arcade. My parents even surprised us and let us play a few rounds of laser tag. It was awesome. I couldn't have asked for a better birthday. I'm so glad the teachers gave us the day off!

When my friends went home I started to feel a bit sad because another birthday was down the tubes and I had to wait a whole year for the next one. Then I remembered that my parents had promised to take Ellie, Jeremy, and me to Splash World to celebrate our birthdays. That was part of their Rosh Hashanah "box of T'shuvah." My parents usually only take us to educational places like museums, art galleries, and historical places.

Don't get me wrong, I love going on the day trips they plan for us. My siblings, on the other hand, were pretty darned excited when Mom and Dad announced that they were going to break with tradition and take us to a water park. Since I like water slides about as much as I like amusement park rides, I wasn't so thrilled with the whole idea but I think I'll still manage to have a good time there. I'm planning on shooting hoops in the water basketball area, maybe swimming a little, and hanging out in the arcade a lot. At least I still have more birthday celebrating to look forward to.

So aside from the batting cages it was a pretty uneventful weekend, other than the usual, going to shul on Shabbat and playing with my friends. That is, until Sunday. Sundays are typically busy days for our family. When we're not doing our homework we're usually rushing off to activities, birthday parties, and family events. Mom runs a lot of errands on Sundays because she's always busy in her studio during the week. She makes fancy invitations and even does some calligraphy. Right now she's working on a *ketubah,* which is an artistic Jewish wedding contract, for Aunt Rachel and Uncle David's wedding next month. (Aunt Rachel is my dad's sister. She and Uncle David aren't married yet but we call him "uncle" even though it won't be official for a few more weeks.) On most Sundays, Dad has to work at the store for at least part of the day. When he doesn't, and Mom isn't working under a deadline, and if by some chance we actually do find ourselves with a few free hours, my parents like to try to organize something for us to do as a family.

But before any of that happens, every Sunday morning Ellie, Jeremy and I have Hebrew school at our synagogue, or as we like to call it, "Shul School." We thought that maybe we wouldn't have it this Sunday because the public schools were closed for those teacher meetings, and in the evening it was going to be Sukkot, but I guess they were trying to squeeze one last session in before the holiday.

Ellie and I generally like going to Shul School. Rabbi Green is the rabbi of our synagogue and he's the teacher for our grade. He's really cool. He's not super old like our parents, and he gives us time to hang out with our friends. But when it comes to actually learning, he lets us ask lots of questions and is willing to get sidetracked from his lesson plans as long as we're talking about Jewish topics. The discussions we end up having are often really interesting.

Mom dropped us off in the parking lot of our shul, Ohav Zedek.

"Have a good time, kids," she called out to us as we climbed out of the car. "I'll do my best to pick you up on time but I have a million errands to run before Sukkot. I'm off to the grocery store. Don't panic if I'm a couple of minutes late, okay?" She was looking directly at me when she said that.

"Mom, don't make the soup without me!" Ellie called back to her.

"No problem, sweetie. I have plenty of other items on my list to do first." And with that, Mom revved the engine like a racecar driver. If she hadn't stopped at the exit and put on her turn signal, you'd think she was in the Indy 500 in last place trying to catch up.

Ellie and I walked into shul and down the hall to our classroom. Jeremy went in the other direction with his seventh grade classmates. All of those kids are studying for their bar or bat mitzvah this year. Jeremy's will be in February.

On our way to class I said, "Ellie, we've been so busy this weekend that I haven't had a chance to ask you if you had fun at your sleepover in the sukkah."

"Yeah, we had a blast. I have to admit, though," she said, "we were all expecting you and Ari to play some pranks on us. Thanks for not doing that. I guess eleven is the year for you to finally grow up!"

To tell or not to tell? That was the question. How could the girls possibly not know that we squirted them? There wasn't a single cloud in the sky! How could they not have figured it out? I decided not to tell. I mean, hey, if we could pull off a perfect prank and not even get caught, then that's like living the dream, right?

We continued to our classroom. I assumed we were going to be learning about Sukkot this week. Our family observes a lot of Jewish traditions and sometimes the topics we discuss get boring for me since I know a lot of it already. I was hoping that today would not be one of those days. Boy, did I get my wish.

"*Shalom, yeladim!*" Rabbi Green's booming, cheerful voice rang out as he entered the classroom. (That means "Hello, children!" in Hebrew.) Rabbi Green always sprinkles Hebrew words into everything he teaches so we learn a lot of vocabulary. Not only that, but he always calls us by our Hebrew names in class and even when we see him outside of the synagogue too. The chattering in the room quieted down to a soft hum when Rabbi Green walked in.

In one hand he was holding a *lulav* and an *etrog*, which are the Hebrew words for a palm branch and a fruit that's a like a big, bumpy lemon—two things that are both used during Sukkot. In his other hand he had a portable CD player, which obviously is not part of the ancient tradition! He placed the lulav and etrog on his desk and turned around to plug the machine into an outlet on the wall. Then he started fussing with some buttons on it.

Kids were curiously craning their necks to see what he was doing. Rabbi Green is always up to something. He likes to make a big entrance in one way or another.

He always keeps us guessing and we never know what he's going to do next, but we can almost always count on the fact that whatever he's got planned is going to be fun. Last month, before Rosh Hashanah, he brought in a shofar, a ram's horn. That wasn't such a big deal. The surprise was when he stood up on his desk and started blowing it. We didn't see that one coming! I'd never seen a teacher stand up on a desk like that before. It was really wild!

Music blasted out of the speakers: *"Well, shake it up baby now, shake it up baby, twist and shout, twist and shout."* I knew that song. My parents are big Beatles fans, and I knew it was a Beatles classic. I watched some of the kids start to tap their pencils on their books, wiggle their feet under their desks and bob their heads to the music. *"Come on and work it on out...."*

Then he did it again. Rabbi Green climbed up on his big wooden chair and stepped right up onto his desk! We were in utter shock when he did it last time. Now, it seemed that this was becoming his trademark. Rabbi Green...we definitely don't understand him!

While standing on top of the desk, he bent down and picked up the lulav and etrog. He started dancing wildly, holding the two together, one in each hand, and shaking them in all directions: up, down, left, right, behind him over his shoulder and in front of himself. He did it for a good long time, almost for the entire length of the song. Then he climbed down and hit the "stop" button, bringing the music to an abrupt end. Some kids applauded. Ethan Meyerson started chanting:

"Go Rabbi, go Rabbi, go Rabbi, go Rabbi," which set off a chain reaction and before long the whole class was chanting it with him. Some of us stood up clapping, dancing and shaking around. So Rabbi Green put the music back on and we all started bopping to the song, with Rabbi Green shaking the lulav and etrog at the front of the class and the rest of us "twisting and shouting" by our desks. Some kids stood up and danced on their chairs. Some even climbed up on their desks just like Rabbi Green. It was a zoo in there.

He didn't let the music go on for as long this time. I think seeing kids on top of their desks may have scared him a bit. After all, if he fell off his desk, he'd have no one to blame but himself. If a kid fell off, it would be his responsibility. I got the sense that he felt he had to stop before things got too out of hand.

When Rabbi Green turned the music off, he was huffing and puffing a little. He reached up to the top of his head to re-clip his smiley-face kippah to his dark, bushy hair, because the kippah had flown off and onto the floor when he was wildly throwing his head around with all of his dancing and shaking.

"Well, that was fun!" he said, trying to catch his breath.

Some kids were still shaking, dancing, and goofing around even with the music turned off.

"Okay, let's settle down now," Rabbi Green said. "Time for our lesson."

"Awww," a few of the kids moaned.

"But we were having fun!" whined Abby.

"So, who says we have to stop having fun?" Rabbi Green responded. "C'mon, everybody, it's time for a field trip."

Everyone looked around at one another. We were all completely confused. A chorus of voices chimed in all at once:

"What?" "A field trip?" "I didn't get a permission slip signed." "My mom doesn't know about this." "Where are we going?"

"Don't you trust me?" Rabbi Green asked, pretending to be offended. "Come on, follow me."

We obediently lined up at the front of the room. And I, like the rest of my classmates, followed him into the hall heading out on the mystery field trip, wondering where on earth he was going to take us.

8

Journey to the Center of the Shul

A buzz of excitement, curiosity, and confusion filled the air.

"Are we really going on a field trip?" Mia asked.

Rabbi Green turned and faced us all. I think he could tell that some kids, including me, were puzzled by this surprise.

"Okay, okay, I'll tell you. It's not a find-a-buddy-and-get-on-the-school-bus sort of trip," he explained. "We're just taking a walk to the courtyard. We're going to visit the synagogue sukkah!"

There seemed to be a mixture of relief and disappointment about this news.

We walked through the halls of the education wing of Ohav Zedek, past all the old pictures of students and teachers. The first ones were really old, in black and white. As we continued down the hallway and passed the pictures from the 1970s, the photos in the frames were faded color pictures of kids in some really strange outfits. The farther we walked, the better the color quality became in the pictures. The 1980s were a huge improvement in terms of picture color. (The clothing and hairstyles, on the other hand, were not much better than the 70s. If anything, they got even weirder!) Right as we were about to turn the corner, we passed last year's pictures, which were bright, clear digital prints. I thought about how it was almost like a museum of technology displaying the evolution of photography. I love the way everything always relates back to the scientific world.

Ellie sped up to walk next to me.

"Excited for Sukkot?" she asked.

"Yeah, I guess so," I said, "how about you?"

"Definitely! Omigosh, it's totally my favorite holiday!" she answered all bubbly and excited. "I can't wait to have guests over, make squash soup with Mom, visit Grandma and Grandpa's sukkah, smell the etrog, sleep outside with Dad, and, and what else...? Oh yeah, how could I forget my most favorite part? Decorating the sukkah!"

"I knew you liked it but I had no idea that Sukkot was your favorite holiday," I said.

"Are you kidding me? I love it! I love everything about it. I even love going to the farmers' market to get the cornstalks and pumpkins and gourds. How can you not love this holiday? It's so much fun!"

"I do like it. I like it a lot," I said, almost feeling defensive. "It's nice and it's a lot of fun, but to me it's also almost kind of sad."

"Sad?" Ellie blurted out. "How can you think Sukkot is sad?"

I was getting a little tired of her enthusiasm. I mean, yeah, Sukkot is a cool holiday, but come on, it's not like winning free tickets to the NBA playoffs or even free passes to the planetarium.

"Well," I said, "it's just that when Sukkot is over, the next thing on the agenda is winter. And I don't really love winter. I mean, I like sledding and playing in the snow, but other than that I don't like being cold all the time."

Ellie put her hand up to her ear like she was holding a phone. "Um? Hello? Calling Mr. Crabasaurus!" She hung up the air phone. "What is wrong with you? You have got to get out of downtown Grumpy Town and realize that Sukkot totally rocks! It's the happiest holiday we have," she said. *Who died and made her head cheerleader?* I wondered.

"Joel, look outside," she said pointing out a window as we passed it. "Could those leaves be any more amazing? And the air is so crisp and fresh. Stop worrying about what's coming next and enjoy what we have now." Ellie seemed to be taking this personally for some reason.

Rabbi Green had been walking directly in front of us. When we got to the glass doors that led outside to the courtyard that's in the center of the building, he stopped and turned around to face our group. Ellie and I were so busy talking that we didn't notice and we both bumped right into his chest.

"Oof," all three of us said at once.

"Sorry, Rabbi," Ellie said.

"Yeah, sorry," I added.

"No problem, yeladim. Actually, I stopped because I couldn't help but overhear what you were saying and I wanted to put in my own two cents, if I may," Rabbi Green said, looking a bit sheepish. Maybe he was torn between wanting to admit that he was eavesdropping and using this as one of his "teachable moments."

He looked around at the group. I glanced at Ellie to gauge her reaction. I wasn't sure how I felt about him using our conversation as a starting point for a lesson. Ellie just shrugged her shoulders and looked up at him waiting to hear what he had to say. I was also curious as to where he was going with this.

"Okay everyone, I have a question for you," he began, "but I don't want you to answer here in the hallway. Think about your answers and then we'll discuss them in the sukkah. I want you to think of the four names for the holiday of Sukkot. And more than that, I want you to try to figure out why the holiday has each of those specific names."

It wasn't clear to me how this was "putting his two cents in," but I figured that like everything else with Rabbi Green, it would all make sense soon.

We followed him outside and into the courtyard. Our synagogue is shaped like a "U" and there's a gate on the far side of the grassy area. The sukkah fits neatly right in the courtyard as if it were custom-made for that space, which it probably was.

I glanced upward and saw that it was a blue-sky, cloudless day. I took a deep, deep breath. Ellie was right about that, at least. It really was a nice time of year. Looking up at the trees in the courtyard, I noticed the yellow and brown leaves rattling on their branches and shimmering, creating a warm golden glow around us. We stepped into the huge sukkah. I looked up from inside and could see that they used cornstalks on their roof for the s'chach like we do at home. The bright sunlight streamed in through the s'chach creating alternating patches of light and shadows on the ground inside. The sukkah was enormous. I estimated that you could almost fit an entire tennis court in there.

The walls were decorated with gourds of all shapes and sizes, some bright yellow and others orange or green. Some had bumps and some were smooth. The preschoolers had been hard at work creating construction-paper fruits and vegetables that were tied to colorful strings. They were hanging down from the beams on the roof, swaying in the light breeze that blew through the sukkah. Two big signs faced one another on the side walls. One said, "*Chag Sameach!*" in Hebrew and underneath was written the translation: "Happy Holiday!" Across the way, the other sign read, "*V'samachta, b'chageicha!*" and below that was its translation: "Be happy in your festival!"

In each corner of the sukkah were bales of hay and gigantic bundles of cornstalks. Rabbi Green asked us to sit down in the circle of chairs that was all set up and waiting for us in the middle of the sukkah.

Knowing our teacher, I was sure we were in for an interesting time. What I didn't know was just how interesting it would turn out to be.

9

The Name Game

Okay, let's talk about the four names we have for the holiday," Rabbi Green began while looking around the circle at sixteen fifth-grade faces. "I'll give you a freebie. The first one is simply Sukkot," he said grinning.

"Duh!" a bunch of kids called out laughing.

"All right, all right," he said, "as you also no doubt know, Sukkot means booths, like the one we're sitting in. So, what other names did you come up with?"

Know-It-All-Hannah's hand popped up even before the rabbi finished asking the question. Ethan Meyerson raised his hand too, with, I noticed, a sly grin on his face. That guy always has some smart aleck comment to make.

Rabbi Green called on Ethan, probably for the entertainment value. We all assumed that Hannah knew the answer.

"In our house, we call it 'The Jabba Holiday'," Ethan shared, looking around at us for a reaction. Ari and I looked at each other and smiled because we both got Ethan's Star Wars reference.

"Cute, *Eitan*. It's certainly not one of the official names we have for Sukkot but it works for me," Rabbi Green acknowledged with a smile, clearly also getting the joke. Then, without making a big deal out of

Ethan's wisecrack he turned to Know-It-All-Hannah. "Chana, did you have an answer?"

"*Chag Ha'Asif*," she said while pushing her glasses up her skinny nose.

"Very nice. Now, do you know what it means?"

Hannah looked around at everyone, making sure that she had our undivided attention. "Yes I do, Rabbi. It means the Gathering or Harvest Holiday because in the time when the Temple in Jerusalem was around, the Jewish people were farmers and they would gather their crops at the end of the growing season and bring gifts of their produce to the Temple."

"*Yafeh m'od!* Very nice, Chana!"

Know-It-All-Hannah sat prissily in her seat letting out a little sigh as if to indicate to all of us that this question was simply too easy for her.

"Any other names?" Rabbi Green asked.

I raised my hand. Hannah gave me a dirty look as if I did something wrong. What? Is she the only one allowed to know anything?

"Yes, *Yoel*?"

"*Z'man Simchateinu*," I answered. "It means the Time of our Happiness, but to be honest with you, I'm not sure that I'm all that happy about it."

"Yes, that's what I heard you saying in the hallway," the rabbi responded. "You're unhappy that right after Sukkot winter will be close at hand, correct?"

"Yes," I said politely, even though I was still kind of annoyed that he had been listening in on our conversation.

"So, why then do you suppose it's called our 'time of great happiness,' Yoel? Why do you think Sukkot is called Z'man Simchateinu?" Rabbi Green asked with a hint of a gleam in his eye.

"You know, it's not winter everywhere," Hannah remarked. "In Australia they're heading into summer. For them it really is their time of joy!"

"True enough," Rabbi Green agreed. "But as you know, the holiday isn't based on the weather patterns in Australia or in the United States, for that matter. If anything, they are heading into winter in Israel, which is their rainy season. But that's not exactly what I'm looking for."

I glanced over at Hannah who looked like she had been punched in the stomach. Know-It-All-Hannah? The wrong answer? Unheard of!

"Come on kids, think," the rabbi prodded. "Why is this called Z'man Simchateinu?"

"Because some of our parents let us get more time out of school?" Ethan quipped.

"Because it's, like, the *greatest* holiday ever!" exclaimed my overly pepped-up sister. All she was missing were the pom-poms and a megaphone.

"Maybe because now that Yom Kippur is over, we don't have to fast anymore?" I ventured quietly. It seemed like a dumb answer but it just popped out. In all honesty, I was really glad to be done with fasting for another year. Actually, Ellie and I didn't fast all day. We won't do that until after we turn thirteen and I have my bar mitzvah and she has her bat mitzvah, but I did fast until three in the afternoon. That's my personal best!

"Yoel, you're on the right track!" Rabbi Green said excitedly.

"Really?" I was surprised to hear that. I wasn't trying to be a smart aleck like Ethan but I was only half serious with my answer.

"Yes!" Rabbi Green said. "And before I explain how you're on the right track, I'm going to throw in another question first. Can anyone tell me the fourth and final name of *The Holiday*?" he asked emphasizing the last two words.

There was an awkward silence for a few seconds until both Mia and Jenna simultaneously exclaimed, "Oh! I get it!"

Rabbi Green nodded at Jenna, giving her permission to go first.

"Jabba the Hutt, from Star Wars! Because this is like a Hut Holiday! That's so funny," she said directly to Ethan.

We all sat there dumbfounded.

"Um, talk about a delayed reaction. What planet were you on, Jenna? " Ethan shot back at her.

"Alrighty then," Rabbi Green said. "Yes, it's a hut holiday. It was indeed a cute play on words. Thanks for helping us relive our good times from ten minutes ago, Jenna. Now, back to the fourth name of Sukkot. Mia?"

"It's *HaChag*, which means *The* Festival or *The* Holiday, right?"

"You got it! And do you know why it's called The Holiday, capital 'T' and capital 'H'?"

We all sat there looking around at one another, waiting to see who knew the answer. Ultimately, we each ended up looking right at Hannah, who, shockingly, was quiet. She just shrugged her shoulders and looked a bit shell-shocked. Not knowing information seemed to be a feeling she'd never encountered before. I almost even felt sorry for her. Almost.

Out of habit, some of us turned to Ethan, expecting one of his sarcastic or witty comments to cut into the uncomfortable silence. Even he had nothing to say.

We all just looked at Rabbi Green with glazed-over expressions.

"Well, don't all answer at once," he chuckled. "Would you like me to tell you?"

"It would be the highlight of my weekend." Finally! It was good to see that Ethan was back in his usual form.

"Okay," Rabbi Green began. "You can think of 'The Holiday' as a big vacation. First of all, as Chana said, back in the days of the Temple in Jerusalem, people used to flock there at this time. They had just finished the intense days of Rosh Hashanah and Yom Kippur and now it was time to bring their harvests and to celebrate. The days were filled with rituals and the evenings were filled with great rejoicing."

Ethan jumped in, "In other words, it was time to party!"

"Precisely, Eitan," Rabbi Green said. "And as to Yoel's comment, we recently finished Yom Kippur, our most solemn and serious day of the year. We took a look back at all of our wrongdoings, all the mistakes we've made, and the ways we might have hurt others. It's hard to think that we're not perfect and to accept our faults. But now we're starting out with a clean slate. We have a fresh new year ahead of us. What a gift! What a joy! So now it's time for us to celebrate. Or as you so eloquently put it, Eitan, it's time to party!" His enthusiasm was in competition with my sister's. "You see, Yoel, your answer really was on the right track."

"Oh. Okay, cool," was all I could think to say in response.

"And speaking of cool," Rabbi Green went on, "the weather reports say that it is going to be a bit chilly at night, but warm during the day all week long, so if you're going to be in a sukkah at night, be sure to bundle up. Is anyone thinking of sleeping in a sukkah tonight?"

A few scattered hands went up, mine and my sister's included.

"That's great! Here's what I want you to do when you're lying down in your sukkah. I want you to look up at the stars and try to picture yourself as an Israelite wandering in the desert. We've already talked about how this is a harvest holiday but it's also about our history. The sukkah is to remind us of the flimsy shelters that the Israelites had while wandering in the desert for forty years after leaving Egypt. So, I want you to picture yourself as if you are there. It will probably be slightly colder for us than it was for them...."

"Actually, the desert gets really cold at night," Know-It-All-Hannah interrupted. "I believe that it can get down to as low as zero degrees Celsius, or thirty-two degrees Fahrenheit."

I have to admit I knew that too. I hope I don't come across as show-off-y as Hannah does. I love collecting information and scientific knowledge as much as she does, but man, is she ever annoying!

"Duly noted, Chana," Rabbi Green responded diplomatically. I wouldn't have been that nice, but then again, I'm not the rabbi.

Not getting sidetracked by Hannah's weather report, he continued, "Okay, bonus question time. Tell me, yeladim," Rabbi Green went on, "how does Sukkot relate to Passover and Shavuot, the other two Pilgrimage Festivals?"

Not surprisingly, Know-It-All-Hannah's hand sprang up faster than kids running outside for recess at the sound of the dismissal bell. Rabbi Green looked around.

"How about someone other than Chana?" he asked.

"Those are all times when our families get together," a girl named Sydney Stern offered. "We always have everyone over for the Passover seder and in my family we all go to my Uncle Dan and Aunt Susie's house for Sukkot. And at Shavuot time, we get together for blintzes at my grandma's house."

"Those are times we get together to eat," Jenna added. "They're food holidays!"

"Absolutely true," Rabbi Green chuckled. "Don't get me wrong, I love the 'eating holidays,' but what else can you think of?"

A kid named Jonah Segal raised his hand. "Aren't those the three times of the year that the Israelites made a pilgrimage to the Temple in Jerusalem?"

"The *Shalosh Regalim*," Hannah called out enthusiastically, not able to contain herself. "Shalosh means three and Regalim means feet, it was the three times the Israelites traveled by foot to Jerusalem."

"Maybe she should make a pilgrimage out of here," Ari whispered to me out of the corner of his mouth. I snickered quietly.

"*M'tzuyan!* Excellent!" Rabbi Green beamed. "Now, super-duper, brain-buster bonus question: How do the three *Chagim*, the three Festivals, all relate to one another?

I glanced over at Hannah. She reminded me of a wind-up toy, fully wound, with someone holding the crank and about to let go. She looked like she was ready to erupt with excitement over this brain challenge. But at the same time, she didn't seem to have the answer yet. I could tell she was thinking pretty hard about it by the way she scrunched up her mouth and wriggled her ankle under her chair. I could see that she wanted so badly to be the first one to come up with the answer. However, no one said anything.

"How about if I give you a little hint," the rabbi said being generous. "Think about the holidays in historical order."

I sat there for a couple of moments trying to put the pieces together like a puzzle in my brain. Then I got it and raised my hand.

"Okay, Yoel, impress me!" Rabbi Green winked at me. The way Hannah sneered at me you'd think I had just kidnapped her kitten or something.

"Well, Passover is when the Israelites were freed from slavery in Egypt. Once they were free, they needed some guidance and rules, which is what they got on Shavuot when they made it to Mount Sinai and were given the Torah. Then Sukkot is about the forty years after that when they wandered in the desert and lived in tents before arriving in Israel. It's kind of like one long continuous story," I realized.

"*Tov me'od!* Very good, Yoel! You guys are on a roll today!" Rabbi Green's smile was so big that he looked like he was going to explode with pride.

Just as Rabbi Green was about to say something else, a rattling noise distracted us. Out of the corner of my eye, I noticed that a cornstalk in the back corner appeared to be shaking.

The discussion came to an abrupt halt and seventeen pairs of eyes transfixed on the quaking cornstalk. With a mixture of surprise, terror, and excitement we watched the bundle of corn tremble. *What's going on?* I wondered along with my classmates.

10

Hey! That Cornstalk's Alive!

It's alive!" Ethan yelled in a Frankenstein-type voice, pointing at the moving bundle.

Sure enough, it was moving! There was no wind, so it seemed pretty clear that something was definitely back there. I assumed it was a mouse or a squirrel or something. Maybe even a rabbit. All the kids got excited about this turn of events. Logically it didn't make sense to be frightened and yet many kids were freaking out. For a minute, the thought of a tiger running away from the zoo did pass through my brain but I quickly dismissed that one. What were the chances of a tiger escaping and hiding in our sukkah? The probability was pretty slim.

"It's a haunted sukkah!" Adam Fisher called out and started to make spooky ghost-like noises.

There was a bit of pandemonium. Some kids seemed to be enjoying the excitement while others actually looked scared. Abby and Ellie clung to each other as they watched the shaking cornstalk. Sydney Stern climbed up on top of her chair and shrieked.

Then the cornstalk fell over with a huge crash. The noise startled me so much that I actually jumped out of my seat. A few kids gasped. We were shocked by what we saw.

"Oh my goodness!" Mia shouted. "Look!" She got up and ran to the back corner.

"What is it?" Matthew Steinberg asked.

"Let me see! Let me see!" a bunch of kids called out. We all crowded around to see what was going on in the corner. To our great surprise, the source of all the mayhem was nothing more than a little, tiny, skinny puppy cowering against the back wall of the sukkah. It was shaking like crazy. I assumed it was trembling because it was scared. It was warm and sunny out so I couldn't imagine that it was cold.

"Okay, okay, let's see what we have here," Rabbi Green said as he made his way through the crowd of kids. He bent down and looked at the terrified dog from a few feet away. He sat down on the ground right in the spot where he was, nice pants and all, being sure to keep a safe distance from the frightened animal. He spoke softly in an assuring voice to let the puppy know that he didn't want to hurt it.

The dog cringed where it was, eyeing Rabbi Green with a look that seemed to be a cross between fear and hope.

"Where'd you come from, little one?" he asked in a soothing voice. The dog sniffed the ground where it was standing and ever so cautiously took a couple of steps closer to Rabbi Green.

"Yeladim," he said to us, "I don't see a collar around this dog's neck, so we don't know if it's a stray or if it's lost or what the story is. I don't want you all to crowd around and scare it." We each took a baby step backwards. I figured that I wasn't the only one who didn't want to move too far away. This was both exciting and unusual. But we also knew that Rabbi Green was right and that we had to be careful because we didn't want the puppy to get panicky and act out aggressively.

Rabbi Green remained in his spot with his legs crossed like a kid sitting in class listening to a story being read aloud by a teacher. He spoke in a soft, gentle voice, keeping his eyes on the dog but directing his speech to us.

"Yeladim, I also want you to understand that you should never approach an unfamiliar dog. Even if she or he has a collar on, they could still get scared and bite you. This is why I'm waiting right here."

We all watched, anxiously waiting to see what would happen. The tiny dog inched its way closer and closer to Rabbi Green's leg. It moved so slowly that we could hardly tell that it was moving at all. It would sniff, step, and look up cautiously. The dog repeated this pattern over and over until it finally reached the rabbi. At that point, it began to sniff his khakis, right near the front pocket.

"Hmm, no collar, no tag, nothing to indicate that this dog has a home," he said, inspecting the dog's furry neck. Eventually, the little animal gave one final sniff and put its tiny paw on Rabbi Green's leg. It climbed right up and over him and settled into the space between his legs as he sat pretzel-style. It was as if the five-foot journey from where the puppy started out and the monumental climb over the mountainous leg to this spot took up all of its energy. Rabbi Green delicately reached down and with one finger stroked the fur behind the puppy's brown ears.

After a few minutes, both the tiny dog and the rabbi seemed to be much more comfortable with one another. The dog lifted its tiny head and looked up at Rabbi Green as if to say "Thank you for being so nice!" When it seemed safe, Rabbi Green scooped up the pint-sized puppy and held it so that all four of its white paws and its white belly were facing us. The poor thing was quaking as if it were shivering in a snow bank. "How about if everyone backs up and makes even a bit more room for this little guy."

"I think you mean 'this little gal'," Know-It-All-Hannah corrected the rabbi.

"Indeed, you are right," Rabbi Green admitted, glancing down at the dog's underside, and looking slightly pink in the face.

Rabbi Green cuddled her as if she were a baby, stroking her little head and saying "Shhhh" to comfort her. It seemed to be working because after a while, she wasn't shaking as much as she had been although she still had a frightened look in her big black eyes.

"I think she could use a drink," Rabbi Green said. "Would someone please go to the kitchen and see if we could get a bowl of water?"

Matthew jumped in the air, shouting, "I will, I will!"

"See if they have a little something safe for her to eat too," Rabbi Green added. "They're probably still in there cooking for the big sukkah dinner tomorrow night. Maybe they have a bit of meat of some sort for her."

"Got it," Matthew said as he sprinted out of the sukkah.

Meanwhile, the rest of us stood around the puppy and gawked. She was really cute, despite the look of terror in her eyes. The fur around her eyes and ears was brown. A stripe of white looked like it was drawn between her eyes and down her nose, spreading out to cover her mouth so that the whole lower part of her face was white. Her back was all brown until about halfway down her paws and her fairly long tail, which all ended up white. It kind of looked like someone had poured brown paint on her back and it ran out just as it got halfway down her legs. I didn't know what kind of dog she was, but if "Way Cute" was a breed, that would have been my answer.

It became clear that we weren't going to talk about Sukkot anymore. Besides, class was almost over. We all stared in amazement at this most unexpected visitor as we waited for Matthew to return.

And then we heard it. The puppy let out a little, tiny "yip".

"Hey! I recognize that sound!" I said to Ari who had squeezed in beside me to get a better view.

"Yeah, me too," he said. "That's what we heard the night I stayed over when we were squir—"

I jammed my elbow into him to cut him off before he could finish the word "squirting," since Ellie was standing only a couple of inches away from us.

"What was that for?" he barked angrily at me.

I pointed my chin in Ellie's direction so as not to actually say anything. I bugged my eyes out at him to get the message across.

"What's wrong with you?" Ari asked, not getting my gestures at all.

I mumbled out of the side of my mouth, "Ellie-ay's ight-ray over-ay ere-thay," I communicated in Pig Latin.

"Seriously, dude, what's up with you?"

Boy, was he being dense! I tugged on his shirt to pull him out of the student huddle to a spot in the sukkah that seemed safe enough to talk.

Once we were in the clear I explained, "Ellie was standing right there! I didn't want her to hear you say that we were squirting them."

"Oh!" Ari said, looking like all the pieces were finally fitting together. "You mean she really never figured it out? I can't believe it!"

"She actually *thanked* me today for *not* playing tricks on her and her friends in the sukkah. She was totally expecting us to do something to them."

"Well, we are just that good," Ari said slapping me on the back.

"Yeah we are!" I agreed. "Anyway, I bet this puppy's been wandering around the neighborhood and was in our yard the other day. It sure sounds like the same noise we heard."

We rejoined the group right as Matthew came speed-walking into the sukkah carrying two soup bowls. One was full of water but I couldn't see what was in the second one. He was totally focused on the bowl with the water, concentrating on moving quickly and carefully so as not to splash all the liquid out of it.

"They're cooking up a storm in there," Matthew said. "They gave me a piece of brisket. Do you think she can eat that?"

Rabbi Green chuckled. "Not only do I think she can eat it, I think we're going to spoil her! No one makes brisket like Carol. I wouldn't mind a piece of her brisket myself but I guess I'll have to wait until the dinner tomorrow night."

Rabbi Green set the bowl of water down on the ground in front of the puppy and placed her paws right in front of it. She sniffed hesitantly at first. Then she cautiously stuck her teeny pink tongue into the water. She did it again and then looked up at Rabbi Green and then at the rest of us. We stood there quietly watching her. I guess she felt safe because she put her head back into the bowl and this time began lapping up the water without stopping. She started slowly and then went at it really fast, as if she couldn't get water into her quickly enough, as if she hadn't had anything to drink in days, which I figured could very well have been the case.

Rabbi Green stroked the dog's back while she ignored his touches and focused intently on quenching her thirst.

Ellie turned and whispered to me, "What time is it?"

"Still didn't find your watch?" I asked in return.

"Not yet," she said defensively.

Just as I was about to answer her, Hannah, in her annoyingly piercing voice called out, "Rabbi Green, it's eleven o'clock. We're supposed to be done now. Can we be dismissed?"

"Oh my goodness, I lost track of the time," he said looking at his watch and then up at us. "Yes, of course. Go ahead. *Chag sameach!*"

Hannah said, "Chag sameach" back to Rabbi Green and headed out of the sukkah. I looked around and noticed that no one else budged. It was like we were all frozen in place watching the puppy go to town in the water bowl, which she was now licking—having finished all the water—trying to get every last drop off the sides.

"What are we going to do with her?" Abby asked as Rabbi Green picked up the small chunk of brisket and placed a tiny, pea-sized piece in the bowl.

"Can one of us take her home?" Mia asked. The tiny dog was now practically inside the bowl, gobbling up the meat and looking for more.

"Since she doesn't have a collar or a dog tag or anything, maybe we can keep her as a class mascot!" Ethan offered. "What do you say, Rabbi?"

"All very good questions," he responded, breaking off another tiny piece of meat.

I could smell its sweet aroma and it made my mouth water. *Lucky dog*, I thought. But then when I considered how scared, hungry, and lonely she must have been I took back that thought.

"What *will* we do with her?" Rabbi Green wondered aloud. "I know I can't take her home because my wife is terribly allergic to dogs. In fact, I'd better wash my hands and clean off my pants really well before I head home."

"We can't leave her here in the sukkah," Ellie said. "Even though she seems to have been surviving on her own for a while, we can't just abandon her now that we've found her." Maybe I was wrong about Ellie. Maybe she would take care of a pet—and not lose it. Then again, she still hadn't found that new watch....

Everyone shouted at once. I got caught up in the excitement too and forgot all about my worries that I might be the only one in my family who would take care of her. She was just so cute! And maybe, I hoped, Ellie would come through after all. It wouldn't be so bad if I didn't have to do it alone. It might actually be fun taking the dog for walks and giving her baths. Maybe I could teach her some tricks. The more I thought about it, the more excited I got about the possibility of taking her home. Unfortunately, I wasn't alone in this thought. A bunch of us wanted to take her. There seemed to be some competition over who would get her. Finally, I spoke up.

"How about if we put our names in a hat—or a bowl," I said pointing at the empty bowl on the ground, "and Rabbi Green will pick a name randomly and that person will ask their parents if they can keep the dog, at least temporarily." Yes, I was quite aware that Ellie and I had double the chances of getting picked. Another benefit of being a twin!

"It's actually not a bad idea that Yoel has," Rabbi Green said. "Of course, no matter who gets chosen, they will need to get permission from their parents first. So why don't we pull out several names of people who want to take the puppy home and we'll number them in the order in which they were selected. If child number one's parent says no, then we'll go on to number two and so on. How does that sound?"

We all agreed that that seemed to be the best and most fair way to choose (thank you very much!). Rabbi Green took a pen out of his shirt pocket and a sheet of paper from his binder. He tore the paper into small pieces and was about to jot down names. But before he even got anyone's first initial down, Sydney said, "You can count me out because I can't take her home. My baby brother might eat her or whack her in the head with one of his blocks or something."

I could have predicted what Ari would say.

"I'd love to take her, but there's no way my parents would let any animal into our house," Ari said. True enough. If I'm afraid to step foot in parts of his house, I can't even imagine how they'd react to an animal with dirty paws or fur that sheds.

"Our apartment building doesn't allow pets," Jenna said.

"If I brought another animal into our house, I think the health department would come after us," Micah said. We all laughed.

"I think animals are kind of gross," Dahlia admitted. *Maybe that's why she was so quick to make that dead squirrel comment the other day,* I considered.

With every additional kid who dropped out, I knew that Ellie's and my chances increased.

"Let's try this a different way," Rabbi Green said. "If you would like to participate in the puppy lottery please raise your hand." We all followed his instructions and Rabbi Green passed the papers around to everyone whose hand was up. Then he handed his pen to Adam and told us to pass it around so that we could each write our names down on the pieces of paper. We folded our papers in half and tossed them into the bowl one by one.

"I know it's getting late, so let's do this quickly," Rabbi Green said. I looked down at my watch and noticed that it was already eight minutes after eleven. I was hoping that Mom wouldn't be worrying about us out in the parking lot. Then I remembered that she said she might be a bit late because of all her errands.

Rabbi Green reached into the bowl, swirled the papers around with his hand and pulled out the first name.

We waited with bated breath as he announced the winner.

11

And The Winner Is...

"Matthew Steinberg," Rabbi Green read aloud. It was weird to hear him say Matthew's name in English since he always calls us by our Hebrew names, but he was just reading what was on the paper.

"YES!" Matthew jumped up in the air.

"Okay, now let's pick out a few more names in case *Matan's* parents say no," Rabbi Green said, already putting his hand back into the collection of papers.

"Ellie Silver," he read. I *knew* that the laws of probability were in our favor!

Ellie squealed and hugged me. I hugged her back. We don't usually do that, but we were so caught up in all the excitement that it just happened.

Rabbi Green put his hand back in the bowl. "Next is...Jonah Segal."

He pulled out a couple more names, but Ellie and I stopped listening and started plotting how to approach Mom with this most unexpected proposition in the event that Matthew's parents said no, which we were hoping would be the case.

Once the lottery was done, we all walked through the synagogue toward the front entryway. Rabbi Green held the puppy in his arms. She looked a lot better already but she still seemed frail. I could see her ribs through her thin coat of fur.

I put my hand on Ellie's shoulder to stop her and said, "We need to put a good spin on this. If Matthew's parents say no then we get to ask Mom and we don't want to blow it. It isn't going to be easy to convince her out of nowhere to take a stray dog into our house. Let's figure out what we should say to her."

"Good idea," Ellie said.

I started. "Maybe we should butter her up a bit. You know, tell her she looks really pretty today."

"Give me a break! That's so obvious," Ellie responded. "She'd know that something was up. Plus, did you see what she looked like when she left the house this morning? If I remember correctly, she was wearing grungy jeans with a big hole in the knee, an old, ratty sweatshirt and her hair was in some kind of a messy ponytail. She'd know we were up to something and would probably just laugh and ask what we wanted from her."

"Hmm, good point," I said. "Okay, how about if we offer to help out with all the pre-Sukkot things that need to be done. She seemed pretty frazzled when she dropped us off. If we can take her mind off of all that she needs to do and help her out, then she might feel a little happier and a bit more open to a huge request like this."

"I don't know about you, but I was planning to help even without being asked. I can't wait to get started!" Ellie said. "I love this holiday, remember? I am totally excited to decorate the sukkah and get ready when we get home."

"Okay, fine. But we still need to handle this the right way. What else should we say to her?" I asked.

"How about if we play up the whole 'doing a mitz-vah' thing? She can't possibly resist that one," Ellie of-fered.

"Good point," I agreed, "especially if we offer to take care of the puppy ourselves. We should tell her that we *both* plan on being responsible for giving the dog baths, walking and feeding her, and taking good care of her in general." I emphasized the word "both" to make sure that Ellie was truly on board with this and it wouldn't only up to me to care for the dog.

"*Tza'ar ba'alei chayim*," Rabbi Green leaned over and said to us. What was with this guy? How and why was he listening to our hallway conversations all the time? Even though his "two cents" were both interest-ing and helpful, I was finding his eavesdropping a little unsettling. But I didn't want to be rude. Plus, I had no idea what he was saying to us.

"Excuse me?" I said politely, trying to hide my frus-tration with his butting into our conversation.

"*Tza'ar ba'alei chayim*," he repeated. "It's the Jew-ish prohibition against unnecessary cruelty to animals. There are many references in the Torah and the Tal-mud as to how we should treat our furry friends. We are repeatedly taught not to treat animals cruelly but even more than that we are responsible for actually taking care of them. That's something that no one can argue with."

"Ooh, good one, Rabbi! That's a point that our mom will really buy into," Ellie exclaimed, not seeming to mind his interfering. "How do you say that again?"

"*Tza'ar ba'alei chayim*," he said a third time. "Let's break it up into pieces. First is *Tza'ar*, kind of like a tzar, a Russian ruler. Next is *Ba'alei*," he said, pausing and looking up to the ceiling as if an answer might fall down from there. "*Ba'alei,* ummm, I don't know how to help you remember that one."

"Like a sheep at the ballet?" I jumped in with a joke. "The Baa ballet, the Baa-lay!"

Ellie rolled her eyes at me. She's not a huge fan of my jokes. But hey, I didn't earn the name Jokin' Joel for nothing.

"Sure, that works," he said. "And finally, *chayim,* like how we say *L'chayim,* to life! Put it all together and it is *Tza'ar ba'alei chayim.* You try it."

We both did our best to say it correctly. We figured that the mitzvah of caring for animals would sell Mom on the idea. She'd be so impressed with us for knowing that expression.

Ellie and I practiced saying, "*Tza'ar ba'alei chayim*" as we walked down the hall together until we got to the front entryway.

There were far fewer cars in the parking lot than usual since we were so late getting out of class. Most of the other kids had left already. Jeremy was leaning against a tree in front of the building with his cell phone in his hands, texting. He glanced up and scoped the parking lot with a severely annoyed look on his face. All the other older kids were already waiting in their parents' cars but Mom hadn't arrived yet.

We watched Matthew walk over to the passenger side of his mom's minivan. Rabbi Green stood by the front doors of the shul with the puppy still nestled in his arms. The dog started squirming and jumped out of his arms. We were surprised to see her "do her business" by a bush. How did she know how to do that already? She looked like she was just a baby. I wondered if dogs instinctively know not to pee on the person who is caring for them. Doubtful. I was also kind of surprised that she was able to go at all since she had probably been fairly dehydrated. I guess that huge bowl of water went right through her. In any case, when she was done, she looked up at Rabbi Green with her sad eyes, requesting in her non-verbal way for him to pick her up again, which is exactly what he did.

Matthew poked his head into the open window. We couldn't hear what he said but we definitely heard his mom.

"What? Are you kidding me? I can barely keep track of three kids! How do you expect me to add a puppy to the list? You've *got* to be kidding!" she said, breaking into a laugh. I think she thought he really was joking.

Ellie and I looked at each other hopefully. Of course, I could totally imagine Mom using the same argument on us. Ellie crossed her fingers and discreetly tucked her hands under her chin. I don't believe in superstitions or lucky charms, so I just closed my eyes and hoped really hard. "*Please, please, please, please,*" I whispered under my breath.

At that moment, Mom's car came barreling into the parking lot. Under normal circumstances, I wouldn't have been too happy with her being so late, but as it turned out we couldn't have timed it better had we tried. She pulled in behind the last car in the lineup at the front door. Jeremy made a beeline for the car, opened the front passenger door, and slammed it as he sat down. Ellie and I stayed at the front doors to see what would happen.

Matthew seemed to be going into begging mode. Again, we couldn't hear him, but his body language told us that he was pleading with his mom as he was hunched over the window hiding his face inside the interior of the car. Ellie and I looked at each other hopefully. If Matthew's mom turned him down, we were the next ones up to bat—and we were going for a homerun!

Some of the parents, including Mom, turned off their engines and got out of their cars once it became clear that something out of the ordinary was going on. Jeremy stayed in the car, reached over across the front seat, and started honking the horn. Patience is not one of his strong points.

"YaYa and YoYo!" Mom called across the parking lot as she approached us. Ellie and I cringed. She knows she's not supposed to call us that outside of the house. "What's going on? Come on, we need to go. I still have a ton of things to do before Sukkot begins and there's hardly any time left."

"Mom, we need to talk to you for a sec," Ellie said as Mom joined us by the front door.

"Is everything okay?" she asked with an odd combination of worry and impatience in her voice.

"Well, yes and no," I answered. "We're fine, but we met someone who's in trouble and may need our help."

"What? Who? What are you talking about?" Mom looked around curiously, a note of anxiousness caught in her voice.

"She looks like she's only a few months old and she can't help herself," I started.

"What? Oh my goodness!" Mom gasped.

"We don't know exactly how old she is, or where she came from, but we found her in the shul's sukkah," Ellie said.

"She's scared and needs someone to take care of her," I added.

"You found a BABY in the sukkah? Oh my goodness!" she repeated, "Where's her mother? We should call the police! Where's Rabbi Green?"

"I'm right here," Rabbi Green said in his comforting, deep voice. "No need to call the police. A veterinarian maybe, but not the police." He walked over to us with the little fur-ball in his hands. The puppy seemed to be getting quite comfortable with him. She was licking his fingers. Either she really liked him or he still tasted like brisket. Or maybe both.

"A puppy? You found a puppy? Oh my goodness! You made it sound like you found a baby—a human baby!" Mom said sounding both shocked and relieved at the same time.

"We don't know where this little one came from, but she was hiding behind a cornstalk in the back corner of the sukkah," Rabbi Green explained. "And now we don't know what to do with her, so we were hoping that someone might be able to take her in, at least for a little while, until we find her owner. She doesn't have a collar or a name tag so we have no idea what her story is."

Mom lifted her sunglasses and set them on top of her head so she could get a better look. She gently showed the dog the back of her hand, waiting to see if she'd sniff her, which eventually she did. Mom slowly reached over to pet the dog who really was irresistible. Then our mother started to make little cooing sounds and talking to the dog as if she was an infant. "Oh my goodness. Who's a sweet girl? Who's a sweet girl? You are. Yes you are...." She was like putty in our hands. I smiled at Ellie and she smiled right back. This was going much better than I had anticipated.

Jeremy blasted the car horn repeatedly. HONK, HONK, HONK, HONK! Did he think we couldn't hear him? Mom put her pointer finger in the air, signaling to him that we'd just be another minute.

"Either someone is worried sick over this little one, or they should be locked up for negligence. May I?" Mom asked, reaching for the tiny dog, who wriggled a bit, not wanting to leave the comfort and safety of Rabbi Green's hold. The rabbi passed her over and Mom practically melted right there on the sidewalk. I never saw her like that before.

Matthew came back looking very disappointed. Shoulders slumped, he reported to us that which we had already heard. His mom said, in no uncertain terms, no. This was our big chance.

Ellie and I geared up for our turn to beg.

"Mom, do you think...." I started. But I was quickly interrupted.

"Well, who is going to take care of this sweet little thing?" Mom asked looking up at the rabbi and petting the puppy at the same time. The puppy seemed to sense Mom's kind nature and nuzzled into her arms as she had with Rabbi Green.

"Well, actually Mom," Ellie took a turn trying to speak, "we were thinking—"

"I cannot believe that someone would just send a puppy off on its own. She must be lost. Oh you poor baby! Who do you belong to? Where did you come from?"

"Um, Mom?" I tried again, "Ellie and I were wondering, well, hoping actually—"

Again, my mother cut me off. "Rabbi Green, do you think it would be okay if we took her home with us? We'll keep an eye on her until we hear about an owner." Then she turned back to her new best friend and started talking in that baby voice again, "You need someone to take care of you. Don't you? Yes you do. Yes you do!"

"That would be wonderful!" Rabbi Green responded. "Are you sure it's no trouble?"

"Oh my goodness! No trouble at all! Right kids?" she asked, barely glancing at us. I was kind of surprised that she even remembered we were standing there because she was so lost in the puppy's spell. She was in love!

"Are you serious? We would love to take her home!" I said, not believing how ridiculously easy this was. We didn't even have to mention that whole sheep ballet thing! I had no idea that Mom was such an animal lover. We'd never had any pets in our home other than a goldfish that I won at a Purim carnival in second grade. (Poor Gefilte, he only survived for three weeks. But it was a good twenty-one days.) Had I known this, I might have asked for a dog a long time ago.

"We were hoping you'd say yes! Do you think Dad will be okay with this?" Ellie asked.

"I think he'll have to be," she said in her silly voice, more to the dog than to us. She started making kissy-lips at the puppy. "Won't he? Won't he? Yes he will! Oh he most certainly will!" The puppy, despite being weak and frail, managed to wag her tail at the sound of Mom's voice.

Jeremy blared the car horn again for a few more seconds this time. Not only did Mom not notice the horn, it was as if the rest of the world just disappeared around her. She kept coddling the dog, "Oh, you poor thing! You must be so hungry. We're going to take you home and give you a bath and get you something to eat and...."

"Hey Mom," Ellie jumped in, "speaking of things to eat, are we still going to make the squash soup when we get home?"

There was a visible shift as Mom blinked, re-entered the real world, and acknowledged us. "Oh, honey, I don't know!" She said in her normal Mom voice (thank goodness!), finally looking up at us. Let's start by going home and sharing the news with Dad. We might have to adjust our plans a bit this week."

"What do you mean? We aren't going to do Sukkot?" I asked not believing what I was hearing. Like I said, I don't like it when plans change. And we always celebrate Sukkot. Plus, the sukkah was already up, and we'd invited people to come over for meals in the sukkah. We couldn't just cancel everything.

"Oh no, no, no! Of course we'll celebrate Sukkot. It just looks like we're going to have another guest in the sukkah this year. I meant that we may have to do things a little differently for these first couple of days so that we can take care of this puppy. Here, you take her, YoYo," she said, passing her over to me. Again, I reflexively winced at her using my private nickname in public.

Normally I'm not a big fan of changing plans midway but in this case it was totally worth it since we were able to take the puppy home. Given Mom's unexpected response, I was curious to see how my dad and my brother were going to react. Well, we were about to see how Jeremy was going to take the news. We headed for our very loud car (Jeremy was now leaning on the horn, full force) with the puppy in my arms.

"I apologize in advance for the guy you're about to meet," I said to the unsuspecting animal in my arms while covering her ears from the horn noise.

This should be interesting, I thought, as Ellie opened the door and we climbed into the back seat of the car.

12

In the Mood for Food

Jeremy didn't hear us get into the car thanks to the racket he was making with the horn. He wasn't even watching to see if we were coming. He was looking down at his phone, texting with one hand, and honking at the same time with the other. When the car doors slammed, he finally let up on the horn. Interestingly, he didn't notice the puppy since he didn't bother looking back at us. Instead, he kept his head down, gazing intently at his phone and chuckling. I figured that he was probably flirting with Ilana again.

"What the heck?" he called out all of a sudden. "Who stinks? YoYo, when's the last time you took a shower, man?"

Ellie thought this was absolutely hysterical. "Yeah, YoYo, isn't this your month to take a shower?"

"No, seriously dude, you smell like an animal," Jeremy said, finally turning around. "Hey! Whoa! What's that?" He pointed at the dog.

"It's called a puppy," I said, mocking him.

"Funny one, Dorkus. I know it's a puppy. Why are you holding a puppy and who does he belong to?" he asked.

"We don't know," I answered, ruffling the fur behind her ears. "We found *her* hiding and scared in the sukkah during our lesson with Rabbi Green today."

"It looks like a boy dog. How do you know it's not a 'he'?" Jeremy asked.

Both Ellie and I shot him a look as if to say, "Are you for real?"

"Oh, yeah, I get it." He said turning away, red in the face. "Does Dad know?" he asked facing the front windshield.

"Not yet," Mom replied. "She's going to spend a couple of days with us since tonight is the start of Sukkot and we won't be able to look for her owner until Wednesday. Tuesday night at the very earliest."

"But if we can't find the owner, will we be able to keep her?" I asked hopefully.

"Well, that's something that we definitely need to discuss as a family with Dad," Mom said. "I'm not saying yes and I'm not saying no. This is a definite 'we'll see' situation."

I looked across the seat at Ellie and shot her a look as if to say, "At least it's not a definite 'no'." She smiled and nodded in agreement.

Mom started driving out of the parking lot. "Okay, kids," she said, "I still need to stop by the farmers' market to get a few more items for the sukkah. We also need to get some dog food for our little guest. Then we'll go home and feed her and clean her up. Will you guys help me out with all this?"

"Absolutely!" Ellie and I said in unison. (We do that sometimes. Twin thing.)

"Great," Mom said. "How about you, Jay? What do you think about this little cutie joining us for Sukkot?"

"It's okay, I guess," he mumbled, seeming to be just as interested in this topic as he would be in an advanced college-level astrophysics lecture (which, by the way, I think might be sort of fascinating). Then in a complete reversal of direction, his face lit up and he said, "Hey, do you think I could maybe invite a friend or two over to meet her?"

Mom looked at him curiously. "Hmm, that was an interesting turnaround. Any friends in particular?"

"Like, maybe a certain girl?" Ellie teased.

"With the initials IG?" I added tauntingly.

"Shut up!" he yelled, his face rapidly turning as red as a ketchup bottle. He slumped down in his seat trying to hide his embarrassment.

"Jeremy!" Mom scolded, "I don't like you talking like that. If I hear you say that again, it will be a week without any screen time whatsoever for you. Got it?"

"Sorry," he grumbled, and then practically whined to Mom, "but why is it okay for them to pick on me?"

"You're right, they shouldn't tease you. But you also need to watch how you speak." She looked at us through the rearview mirror. "YaYa and YoYo, you were definitely antagonizing him. Please stop it and apologize to your brother." It feels like she says this a lot to each one of us.

"Sorry," we said in unison again, much like how Jeremy just said it to Mom.

"As to your question, yes, you may certainly invite a friend or two over to meet her but please make sure they keep their distance until we know that the puppy is in good health. Remember, we really don't know what's going to happen next. I don't know how your father is going to react to this turn of events. Nor do we know if she has an owner. Before we all get too attached, let's agree to take good care of her for a few days, until we can figure out what the situation is."

"But if it turns out that she doesn't have an owner, and you and Dad agree that it's okay, then we can keep her?" Ellie asked, not hiding her excitement.

"You guys just asked me this two minutes ago! I'm sticking with my 'we'll see' answer," was all Mom was willing to give us.

Once we were on the highway, I held the tiny dog up to the window so she could see outside. She had her two back paws on my arm and her front paws up in front of the window. She poked her small, wet nose against the glass and gave a little sniff. Her long tail started wagging a bit. She appeared to be a lot happier now than when she was in the sukkah. She had seemed so frightened and weak back then. I was really glad that she wasn't afraid of us and was willing to trust us. The farther we drove, the more freely her tail wagged, which was great until it started whacking me in the face!

"What do you think we should call her?" I asked, dodging the swinging tail.

"Oh no, stop right there," Mom jumped in. "We're not giving her a name. Not yet. Not until we know that we can keep her."

Ellie and I beamed at each other. We both heard that last part and liked the way it sounded.

Mom continued, "If we name her, it will make us feel that much more attached to her. And if she does have an owner, it will be that much more difficult to say goodbye."

"How about if we just call her Puppy, with a capital P," Ellie suggested, "at least for now?"

"Yeah, Mom," I agreed. "It's better than referring to her as *the puppy* or just *the dog*."

"Fine," Mom gave in. "But I'm warning you guys, don't get too attached. You're only setting yourselves up for possible heartbreak."

After a short drive toward downtown, Mom pulled off of the highway and headed toward the farmers' market. I love this tradition. We go there every year to pick out pumpkins, gourds, and flowers to decorate the sukkah. Mom also gets lots of fresh vegetables there for all the meals that she and Dad prepare for the holiday.

As I held Puppy close to the window so that she could see out, I looked out the window too. We stopped at a red light and I saw a woman across the street on the opposite corner facing the oncoming traffic. She was wearing jeans with a huge hole in the knee with white strings hanging down around the tear from where the denim ripped, and a stained, pink t-shirt. She looked like she was around Mom's age. And even though Mom was also wearing jeans that had some small holes in the knees, they looked like they were supposed to be that way. The woman on the street's pants just looked old and worn out.

Next to the lady, sitting on a turned-over paint bucket, was a little boy who looked like he was a couple of years younger than me. The boy seemed to be really sad and tired. He was banging a stick on the bucket as if it were a large drum. An older girl, probably closer to my age, stood behind the boy. She looked just like him so I figured they were brother and sister. The girl was holding a sign made out of cardboard ripped off of a box that said, "We're hungry. Please help."

It didn't seem to me that anyone else in the car noticed them. Mom was jotting notes and checking things off her "to do" list as we waited at the red light.

Jeremy sat with his feet up on the dashboard, his knees crunched into his chest, balancing a book in which he was completely absorbed. And Ellie was focused on Puppy, stroking her back lightly with her hand. When the light turned green, Mom put her pencil down and drove on toward the farmers' market. I didn't say anything, but I couldn't get the image of that family out of my head even as we drove farther and farther away from them.

When we got to the farmers' market and Mom pulled into a parking space, I stopped thinking about the family long enough to realize that this trip wasn't going to be like our typical yearly outing. We've never done this with a dog in tow before.

"Mom, should I stay here with Puppy?" I asked. "Since we don't have a leash, I don't think it would be such a good idea to walk around with her in our arms. She might jump down and get lost or hurt."

"Or she might eat something that she shouldn't," Ellie added.

"You're right," Mom answered. "How about if the three of you stay here, I'll run over and get what we need, and then hurry back."

"Okay, we'll wait here," Ellie said.

"Actually," I added, thinking of another issue, "what if she needs to go to the bathroom again? We don't want her going in the car."

"Good point," Mom considered. She rummaged around in the car, trying to find something to use as a temporary leash. When she didn't find what she was looking for, she unbuckled the clasp on the woven belt that she had wrapped through the loops in her jeans and pulled it off. She carefully placed it around Puppy's neck and tied it in such a way that the knot wouldn't move and couldn't possibly choke her. "You can stand with her right next to the car. If she needs to go, she can do her business here on the street," Mom said.

"Do I have to stay with them? I like picking out the stuff for the sukkah," Jeremy said with a slight hint of a whine in his voice.

"I don't feel comfortable leaving your brother and sister alone here. I want you guys to stick together," Mom said directly to Jeremy. "I'm sorry that we have to do things a little differently but as I said to YaYa and YoYo before, the situation has changed now that we have this puppy to take care of."

"Fine," Jeremy growled. "Will you bring back some kettle corn from the popcorn guy? I'm starving."

"No you're not!" I roared, as the image of that mom and her kids with their "We're hungry" sign flashed through my mind.

"Who are you to tell me if I'm hungry or not?" Jeremy said angrily.

"You said that you're starving. I'm just saying that there are people in the world that really are. And other living beings too, for that matter." I said looking down at Puppy. Then I said to Mom just before she left, "Mom, don't forget to find something for Puppy to eat. I bet she really *is* starving," I said, glaring sideways at Jeremy, hoping he'd get my point.

"I was thinking the same thing," Mom said. "I'll see if I can get a piece of plain chicken or something for her. That should be okay for her to eat." Then she spoke to Puppy in her baby-puppy-voice. "Hoozagoodgurlll? Hoozagoodgurlll?" she cooed. It took me a few seconds to decipher what she had just said. I finally figured out it was "Who's a good girl?" Then to us, in her normal Mom-voice, she said, "I'll be back ASAP," and she took off walking briskly toward the vendors' stands with empty tote bags slung across her shoulder.

Jeremy opened up his door and called out to Mom, "Don't forget the kettle corn!" Ellie and I rolled our eyes at him, again, synched up to twin-timing.

"Do you guys want anything?" Mom called back to me and Ellie.

"No, thanks," we answered together.

"How is she going to get chicken?" Ellie asked after a few seconds. "They don't have anything kosher here."

"I'm fairly certain that Puppy doesn't keep kosher!" I said, laughing.

"Yeah, I guess," Ellie agreed, "but we do."

"I'm sure it's fine," I said. "It's all part of that sheep ballet thing that Rabbi Green was talking about." I scrunched up my face trying to remember the real name for it. When I remembered I said, "Tza'ar ba'alei chayim. That means it's our job to take care of her and that's the most important thing. She needs to eat. And as I said before, I don't think Puppy observes the laws of *kashrut!*"

I put Puppy on the ground and we stood outside of the car trying to entertain her. I dug around under the seats in our car and luckily found a lonely tennis ball. I rolled it toward her. I could tell, from her eyes, which brightened a bit, and from her tail-wagging, that she wanted to jump on it, but she didn't seem to have enough energy.

"She really needs some food," I noted. "I hope Mom gets back soon."

"Yeah, me too," Jeremy responded sitting sideways with the car door open and his feet resting on the running board. "I'm so hungry I think I'm gonna die."

"Cut it out, Jay!" I barked at him.

"What's your problem?" he growled.

"You need to quit it with the starvation drama," I said. "You are so *not* going to die if you don't get your kettle corn. I actually saw a family begging for food on the street today on our way over here, so I don't think your comments are very funny or very sensitive."

"Well, I *am* hungry," he said in a dull, sort of pouty tone, crossing his arms and not looking at me. I think I got my point across.

After about fifteen minutes, Mom came back lugging a pumpkin in one arm and all of her bags stuffed and overflowing hanging off of her other arm. I walked toward her and took the pumpkin. Ellie held on to the "leash," making sure that Puppy stayed in place and didn't try to run away. As it turned out, she just stayed in her spot on the ground with her little head resting on top of her paws. She didn't make any attempt to escape. I guess she was too weak.

Mom opened up the trunk and we put everything in. Then she pulled out a paper plate and a small package wrapped in aluminum foil from the top of one of the bags. We walked around to the side door where Ellie was standing with Puppy.

As we approached her, Puppy's tail started wagging like crazy. I figured that she could smell the food in the package. Mom bent over and put the paper plate down on the ground in front of her, ripped off a piece of chicken about the size of a dime, and put it on the plate. Then she opened up a small clear plastic deli container of cooked rice.

"How'd you find cooked rice?" I asked

"There's an Asian take-out stand just on the edge of the market. I was going to buy a whole container of rice even though I didn't need so much. They were surprised when I said that was all that I wanted, just rice and nothing else. But I had already found a piece of chicken for her. So I explained why I needed it, telling them all about this sweet puppy that you found. When they heard the story, they just gave me some rice for free. They wanted to help out. Wasn't that generous of them?"

"Yeah, it's nice when people care about others," my sister said, making a subtle jab at our brother. It went right over his head. He was back to texting on his phone, oblivious to the world around him.

Just as Puppy had done before when our class gave her a bowl full of water, she sniffed at the plate of food cautiously and then went at it full throttle. She gobbled up the meat and rice in a fraction of a second and then started whimpering for more. Mom tore off another small piece of chicken, this time closer to the size of a penny and repeated the whole process. Puppy didn't hesitate at all. She dove into that food so fast that I barely saw it touch down on the plate. Mom did this until half the piece of chicken was gone.

"How much can we give her?" I asked.

"I'm not sure. We should probably introduce the food to her kind of slowly," Mom said, "but I do think she should drink more so I got her some water." She went back to the trunk and returned twisting the cap off a water bottle. She took out a second small plastic container just like the one with the rice, and placed it on the ground. No sooner did she pour the water than Puppy practically leaped into the bowl, lapping it up.

While we watched Puppy attacking the water, Mom reached over and handed Jeremy a paper sack full of kettle corn. For that, he rejoined our world.

"Thanks, Mom. You're the best!" he said, immediately stuffing his mouth with popcorn. Needless to say, he didn't offer us any. As I smelled the sweet aroma, my stomach started to growl. I guess I was hungry too but I was so busy with Puppy that I hadn't noticed until just then. I wished I could get a kernel or two to pop into my mouth but I wasn't about to ask the human vacuum cleaner to share any with me. I knew better than that. I also knew we'd be home soon so I could get something to eat then.

When Puppy finished all the water that Mom gave her, we got into the car, buckled up, and headed out.

"Just one more stop," Mom said. "We need to go to the pet store to get some puppy chow because I think that would be the best thing for her to eat. Then we'll go home and get ready for Sukkot."

"And then we get to sell Dad on the concept of our little house guest," Ellie added. We looked at each other, and through our sort of twin-telepathy, I knew just what she was thinking—the same thing that I was: hopefully Puppy will become a family member and not just a temporary guest. We both sighed right along with Puppy, who curled into a tiny ball in my lap and settled in for a contented nap.

13

Special Guests for Sukkot

When we got home, all four of us—Ellie, Jeremy, Mom and I—went out back to the patio together. (Well, actually, all five of us if we include Puppy.) Dad was standing on a ladder inside the sukkah, hanging up a string of white lights that we got during the after-Christmas sales last year. I love that we get to decorate the sukkah and even use those lights. When I was younger I used to be jealous of my Christian friends who got to decorate their Christmas trees. But then my parents pointed out that we *do* get to decorate something—our sukkah!

I started. "Hi, Dad," I said as casually as possible.

"Hey, guys! Where've you been? I could use some help. I was beginning to get worried about you," Dad responded, still busy looping the wire around one of the wall beams and not looking at us.

"I'm sorry, Mark. I had my cell phone on. I wish you would have called me if you were concerned," Mom said.

"I was busy out here," he replied. "But if you guys hadn't returned by the time I finished, that was my plan." He continued wrapping the wire around the beam. He was so focused that he didn't notice that Ellie had Puppy cradled in her arms.

"Well, we've actually had a very unusual day," Mom said.

"Oh yeah?" Dad asked, but not seeming to really be concentrating on what we were saying.

"Yeah, you'll never believe what the kids in Rabbi Green's class found today," Jeremy said.

Ellie and I looked at each other, shocked that Jeremy was actually participating in this discussion. I leaned over and whispered to Ellie, "He must really want to show Puppy off to that Ilana girl." Ellie nodded.

Distractedly, Dad answered, "Um, I don't know what you found. Was it a wallet?"

"Nope, but you're sort of warm," Ellie jumped in. "It's something that someone may be looking for."

"But we're kind of hoping that they aren't," I added quickly.

Dad climbed down from the ladder and moved it to the back wall of the sukkah, glancing, but not really looking at us.

"Hmm," he ventured. "You found something that you're hoping someone won't be looking for? Does that mean you're hoping to keep it?"

"Yes." "Uh huh." "Yep." "Yeah." All four of us answered at once. Even Mom, I noticed. Ellie heard that too and smiled at me.

"Really? Something you all agree on? That's a puzzler. And it's not a wallet? Is it bigger than a breadbox?"

"No," Mom said.

"Is it an expensive watch?" Dad guessed.

"It might be," I answered. Mom, Ellie and Jeremy all looked at me as if I had just announced that I was moving to Peru tomorrow to raise llamas.

"Huh?" Ellie mouthed to me.

I turned my back to Dad, huddled up with the three of them, and whispered, "She might be a *watch dog*! Get it? And for all we know, she could be a pure breed and they're really expensive!"

"Cute, YoYo," Mom said.

"You're an idiot," Jeremy said, swatting at my head, which he missed because I ducked quickly.

"Jeremy! We just talked in the car about watching your language. I expect you to do better," Mom scolded and put her hand out. Jeremy seemed to know exactly what she was getting at.

"Mom!" he whined at her.

"Jeremy, phone," she said in an even tone, with her hand still out.

Jeremy fished into his front pocket, pulled out his cell phone, and begrudgingly placed it in Mom's open palm.

"You'll get this back on Wednesday," Mom said to him. We all knew that that was not much of a punishment since we don't use the phone during a holiday anyway, but her point was made. Jeremy just sort of shrugged an apology.

We all turned back to Dad.

"No, Dad, it's not a watch," Ellie said, resuming the conversation.

"Speaking of which, did you find your watch yet, YaYa?" Jeremy jumped in, clearly trying to add our sister to Mom's "you're-in-trouble" list. It worked.

"What? You lost your brand new watch already? The one that Bubby and Zayde sent you last week?" Mom squeaked. "YaYa, I thought you were going to try harder to keep track of your belongings," Mom said without hiding the disappointment in her voice. Jeremy hid a small, satisfied smirk.

"Um, well, it's not really lost. I just don't know exactly where it is. I know that it's in my room somewhere. I'll find it," Ellie said, simultaneously shooting imaginary darts out of her eyes aimed at Jeremy. Her famous ears started turning a pinkish-red hue.

"Thanks a lot, Jay," she snarled quietly at him.

I leaned over to her and whispered, "I'll help you look for it later if you want. I'm sort of scared to go into that messy room of yours but I'll be brave."

"It's nowhere near as bad as it was before I did my T'shuvah Box when I promised myself I'd keep it neater," Ellie said, defending herself.

"That's true." I gave her that one, but in all honesty her room was still pretty frightening. My sister's not exactly a neat-freak, and I'm guessing that no matter how hard she tries, she never will be.

"Not a watch, Dad. Keep guessing," Ellie said, clearly changing the subject back to one that was more comfortable for her.

"Okay, smaller than a breadbox, something you want to keep, it may be valuable, and it's not a watch? I don't know. Can I give up?" As Dad said that he backed down from the ladder and finally, for the first time since we arrived, turned to really look at us. His eyes swept across all four of us, but after he looked at Ellie, he did a double take and noticed Puppy.

"Is this what you found?" Dad asked in amazement.

"Yes!" Ellie exclaimed. "We found her during our lesson with Rabbi Green out in the shul's sukkah. We don't know how she got there or who she belongs to, if anyone. But someone needed to take care of her and we volunteered to take her in, at least over the first couple of days of Sukkot."

"Until we can find her owner," Mom added quickly.

"Wow! I did not see that one coming. A puppy wasn't anywhere on my possible list of things to guess," Dad said, moving closer to get a better look. "She sure is a cute one, isn't she?" He put his hand backwards in front of Puppy's nose. She carefully sniffed it and then gave one little lick across the back of his hand as if to say she approved.

"I think you've made a new friend, Dad. She likes you," Ellie said.

"Do we know anything at all about her?" he asked.

"We know that we're calling her Puppy with a capital P since we don't know her real name," Ellie said.

"And that she was hiding behind a cornstalk bundle in the sukkah," I added.

"No collar or anything?"

"Nope," Ellie said. "We have no idea where she came from or how she found her way into the courtyard."

"Hmm, that's true," Dad considered. "The only way to get into the courtyard is either through the synagogue building or through the gate on the far side. I wonder if someone put her there on purpose or if she snuck in when the gate was open."

"Yeah, we've been trying to figure it out ourselves," I said. "I thought I heard some little animal noises outside the other night."

"Puppy must have been hangin' in the 'hood," Jeremy added.

"I'll tell you," Dad said, "I'm not so comfortable having a stray dog in the house like this. We don't know anything about her. She may have a disease, she may have fleas, there could be lots of things we should know about." My heart sank. Did this mean that he wouldn't let her stay with us for the next couple of days?

"However," he continued, "she needs a place to stay, so let's figure out a way to take care of her over Sukkot without putting ourselves in harm's way."

Phew!

"I called Nancy Donohue while I was at the farmers' market," Mom reassured him. "You know our neighbor from the PTA, the veterinarian? She said she'd try to stop by tomorrow evening on her way home from work to take a look at Puppy. I agree that we should be careful until we know more about her. In the meantime, maybe we can set up a little 'apartment' for her in the garage. Even if it gets a bit cool out tonight, I think it will be warm enough in there for her."

"That's not a bad idea, Deb," Dad said. "I wonder if any if our neighbors have a kennel we could borrow. How about the Parkers down the street? They have a couple of dogs. Jay, would you run over there and see if they have a kennel or a pet doohickey of some sort that they'd be willing to lend us for a few days?"

And with that Jeremy raced out of the backyard. Couldn't get away from us fast enough, it seemed.

"Do you guys need any help?" Ellie asked our parents.

"I would love some help in the kitchen in a little while. But I have to get a few things organized first. I'll call you when I'm ready for you," Mom said heading into the house.

"I could use some help tossing the cornstalks up on the roof if you guys wouldn't mind," Dad said.

"That's one of my favorite jobs!" I called out, running over to the pile of stalks on the ground.

"Dad, would it be okay for me to put Puppy down and let her run around the yard?" Ellie asked.

"As long as the gate is closed, I don't see why not," Dad said.

Ellie put Puppy down on the ground and joined me at the big stack of stalks that were about to be our sukkah's roof for the week. Puppy sniffed the ground and began exploring this new territory. She looked as tiny as a lone lizard on the big open savannah.

As I watched her sniff around the yard, I noticed a small red thing on the ground. Oh no! It was one of the water balloons that Ari and I threw down the other night before switching to the squirt guns. I knew that I had to find both balloons before anyone else did. If my sister or parents were to find them and if they figured out that I was throwing them, I'd be in huge trouble. And if Puppy found the balloons and tried to eat them, she could choke on them.

I left the pile of cornstalks and ran around the yard pretending that I was playing with Puppy, but I was really searching for the balloons. The red one was easy to find. The green one was a bit harder since it blended in with the lawn but after a few minutes of running around I found it. The red one was broken so I shoved it into the pocket of my jeans. The green one was mostly deflated but still had some water in it. I jumped right on top of it and crushed it. Puppy jumped wildly when she saw me jumping. She thought this was some sort of a game. I sneakily bent down, reached for the green balloon, shook it off and slid it into my pocket. Then I kept jumping to make it look like I was still playing the game.

"YoYo, quit goofing around! Come and help," Ellie called to me.

"Coming," I yelled back. I headed toward the sukkah but Puppy still wanted to play. I knew I had to work on the s'chach, so I thought of a different game to play with her. I'd seen dogs tug on ropes and sticks in their mouths, so I grabbed a cornstalk from the pile and held it out for Puppy to play with, figuring she'd like that.

"Here, girl!" I called.

Puppy's mood changed considerably. She looked at me suspiciously, her body crouching in a way that seemed to communicate that she didn't trust me. That was weird. I tried again.

"Here, girl! C'mon! Come play with the corn!" I shook it around to try to entice her. I really thought she'd come running to tug on the stalk. Instead she whimpered and ran to the opposite end of the yard. She cowered by the fence in the far corner and let out some of those now familiar yips.

"What did I do?" I asked.

"She must be afraid of the cornstalks," Ellie said. "Remember, that's where we found her. I know dogs have a really strong sense of smell. Maybe she recognizes the smell and thinks we're going to leave her behind a cornstalk again."

"Yeah, you're probably right. She must have a bad memory of the smell of corn. Oh! I didn't mean to scare her. I just wanted to play with her." I felt as bad as if I had invited a friend over for an awesome dinner and then served fried tarantulas. I mean, yeah, I like pranks but I would never do anything downright mean. I certainly wasn't intending to scare Puppy.

"Let's just get the s'chach up and when she sees that it's safe, I'm sure she'll come back. Just let her be for now," Ellie said.

And that's precisely what happened. Ellie and I had fun throwing the stalks up in the air like javelins to the top of the sukkah and Puppy watched from a safe distance across the yard. While we were tossing the stalks, I thought of a joke that I read in a joke book a while ago and had saved for this very occasion.

"Hey, YaYa."

"Yeah?"

"How much did the pirate pay for his corn?"

"Is this another one of your dumb jokes?" she asked.

"It's not dumb. Maybe a little 'corny' but not dumb!" I crack myself up! "Come on, guess. How much did the pirate pay for his corn?"

"I don't know. How much?" she said reluctantly.

"A buck an ear! Get it? Buccaneer? Am I funny or what?"

Ellie swatted at me with her cornstalk. "I'm going to go with 'or what'?" I ducked out of the way in time for her to miss me. There seemed to be a lot of attempts at swatting my head that day.

Dad called over from the other side of the sukkah, "Come on, kids. No time for horsing around. We've got to get this sukkah done before sundown."

We continued throwing the cornstalks up on the roof. I love the "thwack" sound they make when they land right on top of the roof beams. Ellie and I had so much fun. Dad seems to know the exact number of cornstalks to get every year because we always have the perfect number—not too many that they cover the whole roof and not too few either. When we sit inside during the day, there's supposed to be more shade than sunlight. And at night, there should be enough open space that we can look up and see the sky and the stars. I went inside to make sure it wasn't too covered up and it looked good.

Sure enough, when all the cornstalks were off the ground and I went back out of the sukkah, Puppy sauntered over to us slowly.

Ellie said, "I'm going inside to help Mom with the soup." Dad and I carried out our big folding table that we keep in the garage and schlep in and out of the sukkah for the duration of the holiday. It was a little tricky carrying the heavy table and watching out for Puppy, who followed us underfoot as we walked across the patio. Once we went inside the sukkah, however, she stopped following and watched us from the doorway. She sat looking into the sukkah without budging, almost as if a wall stood between her and the entrance. I figured that she was once again remembering the place where we found her, which must have been incredibly scary for her.

Jeremy returned from the Parkers' house but he wasn't carrying the kennel. Ben Parker followed behind Jeremy carrying it.

"Hi, Ben," Dad called out to Jeremy's friend.

"Hi," Ben replied. "I came over to see the puppy."

"Do you have any idea who she might belong to?" Dad asked.

"Nope, not a clue. But I heard some kids in the neighborhood saying that they thought they saw a small stray dog wandering around. I didn't realize it was a puppy."

After they spent a few minutes checking out Puppy, Dad asked Jeremy to please help set up for dinner in the sukkah. Ben joined in and the two of them began hauling wooden folding chairs.

Ellie came out and informed us that it was going to be the five of us, plus our grandparents, Aunt Rachel and Soon-To-Be-Uncle David and another couple, the Kaplans, who my parents met at synagogue. So we needed eleven chairs. I went to help them with the carrying and had an idea. I brought out an extra chair.

"Where'd you learn to count, Einstein? We already have eleven chairs," my brother announced.

"We have an extra guest coming tonight," I replied as if he hadn't just tried to insult me.

"Oh, I'm not staying for dinner," Ben said.

"No, I know that," I said.

"Did you put that out for the *Ushpizin?*" Dad asked.

"The who-zin?" Ben asked.

"The Ushpizin," I said. "It's a custom on each night of Sukkot to 'invite' a person from Jewish history to join us in the sukkah. It's like on Passover, when we put out an extra chair for Elijah, some families put out an extra chair for the Ushpizin. The guest of honor tonight, according to tradition, is supposed to be Abraham from the Torah."

"Hey," Ellie jumped in, "how about Sarah? Why are you leaving her out?"

"Ellie, we barely have enough room for one extra chair," I said.

"Yeah," Jeremy mumbled. "What do you want her to do, sit on his lap?" We all laughed.

"Well maybe he sits on her lap," Ellie shot back.

"Whoa, whoa, whoa, whoa, whoa," Dad cut in, "These are our patriarchs and matriarchs we're talking about here. Let's keep it respectful," he said, trying to hide a small grin.

"Actually, Dad," I admitted, "I wasn't bringing the chair out for Ben or for Abraham or for Sarah," I added for Ellie's benefit, "I was bringing the chair out for our other special guest—Puppy!"

Dad chuckled. Puppy remained sitting at the doorway but her tail was wagging happily. I wondered if she was able to tell that we were talking about her and that she was going to be a special guest in the sukkah. That is, if she would be willing to come *into* the sukkah.

I could tell that it was going to be an interesting Sukkot this year.

14

Hospitality Hut

A few hours later, we were all ready for our dinner in the sukkah. Ellie, Jeremy and I had hung up all the decorations just in time. We strung colorful paper chains across the ceiling and tacked up some pictures to the wall—drawings and paintings of fruits and vegetables that each of us had made when we were younger and that Mom had preserved with the cool laminating machine she has in her studio. Dad also drilled some holes into the stems of the gourds that Mom had picked up at the farmers' market and we put strings through them and hung them from the beams on the roof. I always forget from one year to the next how much I enjoy decorating the sukkah. It was so much fun!

Once we finished decorating, we set the table. With the food ready in the kitchen, my parents, siblings, and I gathered on the patio for the annual lighting of the sukkah. I don't know if most families who have a sukkah do this but it's one of our many Silver family traditions. I held Puppy up so she'd get a good view of the exciting light show.

"Is everyone ready?" Dad asked.

"Yes!" we all answered. Even Puppy barked as if on command. I noticed that she seemed so much more chipper now that she'd had some food and water and felt so comfortable around us.

Dad plugged the cord into the electrical outlet on the back of our house. The entire sukkah lit up.

"It looks like a sign on Broadway!" Ellie exclaimed.

"Nice job, everyone!" Mom praised.

"Cool," said Jeremy.

"It's so pretty!" Ellie cheered. "Have I mentioned lately how much I love this holiday?" *Uh oh, here come the pom-poms again,* I thought.

"Nice job with the lights, Dad. It looks really awesome," I added to the compliment chorus.

I gingerly placed Puppy on the ground to see if maybe her sukkah-phobia was decreasing since she was surrounded by people who liked her and were caring for her. I was hoping that she'd realize it wasn't scary or dangerous. She didn't budge but she also didn't run away, which I figured was a good sign. Ellie seemed to pick up on what I was doing and went into the house to get a treat for her. She came back out, went inside the sukkah, squatted down, and put her hand out with a few small pieces of dog food in her open palm. Puppy slowly crouched low to the ground and took a couple of cautious steps into the sukkah. Then she dove for my sister's hand, nipped the food right out of it and ran back outside. Ellie jumped back a little and shook her hand out.

"Did she bite you?" Dad asked concerned.

"No," Ellie said, giggling, "she just startled me, that's all. I'm guessing she just wanted to grab her snack and hightail it out of the sukkah as quickly as possible."

"Ha! Hightail, I get it! Because she has such a high tail! You're starting to pick up on my sense of humor," I said.

"Oh please, YoYo," my sister responded, "I was not trying to make a joke. You're the corny one in the family, not me. Anyway...." She said redirecting us back to Puppy.

I jumped in where she left off. "Anyway, our theory is that she has a bad connection with the sukkah since that was where she was hiding, cold and scared. We're hoping that we can give her enough good experiences here so she'll come around and start to like the sukkah. That was step one."

"As long as no one got hurt," Dad said, seeming to be satisfied but still a bit hesitant.

"I'm fine, Dad, I promise," Ellie said. "I don't think Puppy could hurt anyone—at least not on purpose. She's so sweet!"

"She does seem like a good girl," Dad agreed, "but we still don't know anything about her history, so please be careful."

"We will," Ellie and I both said. Ellie skipped out of the sukkah to go find our number one topic of conversation, who had run around the corner with her prized treat.

Before long our guests began to arrive and they joined us in the backyard. Grandma Ruth and Grandpa Jack, my dad's parents, were first. Behind them entered Aunt Rachel and Uncle David.

"Oh, the sukkah looks lovely!" Grandma said as she made the rounds giving each of us an enormous Grandma-style hug and a big juicy kiss on our cheeks.

"Chag sameach, kids," Grandpa said, pecking each of us on top of our heads, even my parents. I always find it funny that my grandparents refer to my parents as "kids."

After all the greetings were completed, I thought it would be a good time to share our big news with the family.

"Hey everyone, we have something very exciting to share with you!"

Without missing a beat, Grandma turned to Mom, threw her hands on Mom's belly and shrieked, "You're pregnant? You're having a baby? Oh, sweetheart! How wonderful!"

Mom stared at her in disbelief. Actually, I couldn't tell if it was more disbelief or annoyance. She removed her hands and very calmly said, "No, Mom, I'm not pregnant." I like the way my mom calls both her own mother and my dad's mother "Mom."

"You're not? Oh, I thought maybe—" Grandma said, talking to Mom's belly rather than to her face.

"What are you saying? That I look pregnant?" Okay, I could now tell. She was definitely annoyed, bordering on angry.

"No, no, dear," Grandma backtracked. "Well, I have been thinking that lately you've been looking a bit puffy—"

"MOM!" Dad yelled in my mother's defense.

"Well," I said, "you're sort of close because it may possibly involve a new member of our family." I was hoping to rescue everyone from this painfully awkward conversation.

Grandma was still staring at Mom's stomach. Mom definitely looked annoyed now. Had Mom been a balloon, all it would have taken was one more little puff of air to make her pop. With strained calm, she took a deep breath and said, "Ask the kids what they're talking about."

Grandma and Grandpa both turned to me. I pointed at Ellie, who came around the corner of the sukkah carrying Puppy. "Ta-da!" she sang out.

"A puppy!" Grandma exclaimed. "Why'd you tell me that your mother was having a baby?"

"I think you must have jumped to that conclusion, Grandma," I said, trying to be as respectful as possible knowing full well that that was the case. This conversation was getting ridiculous.

We told Grandma and Grandpa all about how we found Puppy in the sukkah at shul school and how we had heard little yips earlier in the week, which we figured out must have been her roaming around the neighborhood.

"Does she have her shots?" Grandpa asked.

"We don't know anything about her," Dad explained. "All we know is that she was alone in the shul's sukkah when YaYa and YoYo's class found her. They volunteered to take care of her over Sukkot. We're going to have a vet take a look at her tomorrow and then after the holiday we'll see what we can figure out."

"And if nobody claims her, we might even get to keep her!" cheerleader Ellie jumped in.

Grandma looked at Aunt Rachel. "*You're* still going to give me some grandchildren, aren't you?"

If Aunt Rachel was annoyed by this prying into personal information she sure did a good job of hiding it.

"How about if we work on getting through the wedding first, Ma!" Aunt Rachel said, laughing. She was in a much better position for Grandma's baby comments than Mom was. After all, she might actually have a baby after she gets married. Or two or three!

Just then, the Kaplans showed up. *Good timing*, I thought. *Better now than during that awkward showdown between Mom and Grandma.* Mom and Dad introduced their new friends to all of us.

"Karen, Scott, we'd like you to meet our family," Dad began. "These are my parents, Jack and Ruth, my sister Rachel, Rachel's fiancé, David, and our kids, Jeremy, Joel and Ellie.

"You can call me Jay," Jeremy said.

"Nice to meet you, Jay," Scott and Karen said together, taking turns shaking Jeremy's hand and then making their way around to everyone. Then to Mom and Dad, Scott said, "Mark and Debbie, thank you so much for inviting us over for dinner in your sukkah tonight. We really appreciate it."

"It's our pleasure," Mom said. Then she explained to everyone, "Karen and Scott just moved to town a couple of weeks ago. We met them after services at the shul's break-the-fast after Yom Kippur."

Scott added, "We moved here for Karen's job and we don't know too many people in town yet."

"Well, welcome to our community!" Grandpa said. "How are you adjusting?"

"No complaints," Karen said. "My job is already keeping me really busy and Scott is looking for a position as an accountant. We're still unpacking and getting settled in but so far, so good. We haven't had much of an opportunity to meet many people, but those we have met have been so friendly and welcoming."

Mom smiled when she heard this.

"I'm so glad," she said. "We always enjoy having guests and making new friends. Plus, have you ever heard of the term 'Hachnasat orchim'?" Both Karen and Scott shook their heads no. Mom continued. "It's the mitzvah of welcoming guests and it's especially encouraged during Sukkot. So your being here is as much a privilege to us as our inviting you. Not to mention that we're just happy to have you over."

"Glad to be able to help!" Scott joked.

"And we have another visitor here tonight too," I said, introducing our new guests to Puppy, who was still hanging out in Ellie's arms. I felt like I had to explain why we were calling her Puppy and not by a "real" name and why she was unwilling to step foot (or paw) into the sukkah.

When Ellie put her down this time, Puppy stayed with us right outside the doorway. She seemed to be slowly warming up to the idea of the sukkah.

Aunt Rachel gravitated toward Karen and the two of them started chatting. I could tell there was an instant connection between them. It's kind of cool when you get to see the moment a new friendship begins, which is what I assumed I was witnessing.

"Well, how about if we get started?" Dad said after a few moments of everyone standing around and schmoozing.

We all made our way into the sukkah. It was a bit crowded with so many people inside, but luckily our sukkah is pretty big and able to fit the large table and all of the chairs, although not much else.

Mom placed two candlesticks with a fresh, white candle standing tall in each holder at the head of the table.

"Can I light the candles, Mom?" Ellie asked.

"Sure," Mom said, handing her the matches.

"I love this holiday! I can't wait to get started!" Pom-pom Girl announced as she struck the match and lit the two candles.

Ellie recited the prayer out loud, *"Baruch atah Adonai, eloheinu melekh ha'olam, asher kid'shanu b'mitzvotav v'tzivanu l'hadlik ner shel yom tov.* Blessed are you, Adonai our God, Ruler of the universe who has sanctified us with your commandments and commanded us to light the festival candles."

Everyone said, "Amen."

"Okay, now let's do the *Kiddush* and the blessings for Sukkot," my father said. He took a glass of wine in his hand and held it up and recited the long blessing over the wine. When he was done, he turned to Grandpa and asked, "Dad would you like to lead us in the sukkah blessings?"

"No, no, son, it's your home and your sukkah, you lead. I'll lead when you come to my house."

"I'll do it!" Ellie volunteered. "I love doing the *brachot* for Sukkot! I love *everything* about this holiday— even saying the blessings!"

Shocking.

"Okay, sweetie, go for it. Joel, do you want to translate the blessings in English?"

"Sure," I agreed, glad to be asked, but not nearly as excited about it as my sister.

Ellie, in her bubbly voice, began, *"Baruch atah Adonai, eloheinu melekh ha'olam asher kid'shanu b'mitzvotav v'tzivanu leishev ba'sukkah."*

My turn, not quite as bubbly. I read from the plaque that was hanging on the wall of the sukkah: "Blessed are you, Adonai, our God, Ruler of the universe, who has sanctified us with your commandments and who has commanded us to dwell in the sukkah."

As we were about to say the *Shehechiyanu* prayer together, I noticed out of the corner of my eye that Puppy had inched her way into the entrance of the sukkah and was sitting and watching us all from inside. We were officially saying the Shehechiyanu prayer because it was the first night of the holiday; it's what we say to thank God for letting us live another year to see this occasion once again. But we also say it when we experience something for the first time, and a small piece of me was also saying it to thank God for letting us have our very first Sukkot with Puppy, even though she wasn't really ours yet. It felt good to at least pretend that she was a part of our family.

We all said together: "*Baruch atah Adonai eloheinu melekh ha'olam shehechiyanu v'kiyimanu v'higiyanu lazman hazeh.* We praise you God, Ruler of the universe, for sustaining us and enabling us to reach this season."

We had a delicious dinner in the sukkah. A light breeze blew through the thin walls making the hanging gourds spin above our heads. The air was getting cool enough for us to wear light jackets and to serve as a reminder to me that winter was on its way. But I took my sister's advice and didn't let that get me down. I enjoyed the company around the table. And unlike in past years, I also enjoyed the company that was now *under* the table licking my leg.

15

Sleeping Under the Stars

We have *got to* invite the Kaplans to the wedding!" Aunt Rachel said to Uncle David as we were cleaning up at the end of the evening. "They are so wonderful. Karen and I already made plans to go out for coffee next week. I really like them."

"I thought we were trying to cut down the invitation list not make it bigger," Uncle David replied, carrying a full stack of plates toward the house.

The two of them disappeared inside while Dad and I carried the big table back out of the sukkah and into the garage.

"Are you sure you want to sleep in the sukkah tonight?" Dad asked. "It's getting a bit chilly out here."

"Definitely!" Ellie shouted, following us into the garage. "It wouldn't be Sukkot if we didn't. It's a tradition!"

"Fine with me, but we'll really need to bundle up," Dad said.

Once we were done clearing the sukkah of the table and chairs, we swept the patio floor and went down to the basement to haul out our sleeping bags. On our way back outside we ran into Mom in the family room.

"Hey, Mom, do you think you might want to join us sleeping out in the sukkah this year?" I asked.

"No thanks," she replied. "I'll stay inside and keep an eye on things in here."

"So will you please tell us why you don't sleep in the sukkah?" Ellie asked. "I don't get it. You come camping with us and you like that."

"It's not about sleeping outside," Mom began. "I love the outdoors and being in nature. It's just that something happened when Aunt Julie and I were little girls and now I can't bring myself to sleep in the sukkah. I've been scarred for life," Mom said in an overly dramatic voice.

"Tell us!" Ellie and I pleaded together.

"No, I don't want to ruin it for you."

"Please!" we begged.

"Fine, I'll tell you if you promise not to let it get in your way of enjoying your special time in the sukkah. I love that you guys sleep out there with Dad."

"We promise!" we said together in one voice.

"Okay," she began. Ellie and I sat down on the couch eager to listen. This was so exciting! We've been waiting *forever* to hear her scary sukkah story.

"When I was about five years old and Aunt Julie was about nine, we were sleeping out in our sukkah with Zayde and Bubby," Mom said. "Aunt Julie thought it would be funny to frighten me, so she started telling me scary stories about raccoons as soon as Bubby and Zayde fell asleep. You wouldn't think that raccoons are really all that terrifying, but each night that we stayed out there, she made up different stories about all sorts of ways the raccoons were going to get me. She told me that they would slink across the very flimsy roof and fall through, right on top of us. Or that they would crawl into our sleeping bags and settle in with us for the night. She even had me convinced that they were going to come and eat our hair while we were sleeping and that we'd wake up bald. It scared the daylights out of me. I had raccoon nightmares for years. And to this day, even though I have never seen a single raccoon in our neighborhood, I just can't do it."

"So you never actually had an encounter with a raccoon?" Ellie clarified.

"No, not even one. And if I thought for a minute that you'd be in any danger, I wouldn't let you sleep out there. I know it's not logical, and it's even a bit silly but I can't bring myself to do it."

"Wait a minute!" I called out. "I thought it was Aunt Rachel who was a troublemaker for Dad when they were kids."

"She was, but so was Aunt Julie," Mom replied. "We each had one in the family."

"Aunt Rachel? A troublemaker?" Dad chimed in while walking past carrying his own sleeping bag and pillows, "She was and still is. She's nothing but trouble, that sister of mine," he quipped. My father and his sister are like kids who never grew up when they're together. To this day he still calls her a troublemaker and she calls him her smelly older brother.

"So you mean to tell me that I got my prankster genes from *both* sides of the family?" I asked, surprised to learn this now, already eleven years into my life. How did I not know this about my Aunt Julie? She always seems so ordinary and grown-up-like. It never occurred to me that she has, or at least had, a mischievous side to her. I needed to have a word with her. *I bet she's got lots of good suggestions for me,* I thought. Aunts...who can understand them? Well, maybe I can, actually!

"Don't get any funny ideas, YoYo," Ellie said as if reading my mind. "You've been so good about not playing tricks on me lately, and I'd like to keep it that way. Plus, don't forget, you promised."

Once again, I was surprised to hear that she and her friends didn't realize that we squirted them in the sukkah the other night.

After saying good night to Mom, we made our way outside. Before getting ready for bed, Ellie and I went out to the garage to take care of Puppy. She was already inside the kennel sleeping, but when we opened the door from the house to the garage she woke up instantly, jumped to her feet, and wagged her tail furiously. I felt bad seeing her in this cage-like contraption, but I knew it was the best thing for everyone. Ellie and I decided to take Puppy for one last walk before we all went to bed. We took the leash that the Parkers had loaned us and hooked Puppy up. Now she was in full happy-dog mode, jumping on us and yipping like crazy. It was amazing how different she was from earlier. She was so peppy now...almost like Ellie.

We walked her along the curb on our street for a few minutes. Puppy's tail wagged happily as she sniffed every blade of grass, every rock, and of course the fire hydrant. I stepped on a small pile of crisp leaves on the sidewalk that made the most satisfying crunch under my feet. After she'd had a decent stroll we returned to the garage to put her back to bed. She did not like this idea one bit. She scratched and clawed at the smooth, gray garage floor, fighting the kennel with every ounce of effort that she had. It broke my heart. I didn't want to put her in there but what choice did we have?

We finally got her inside by putting a little piece of dog food in there. I felt bad tricking her like that. This wasn't the kind of trick that was fun to play but we knew we had to get her in there somehow.

"Good night, Puppy," I said.

"Sweet dreams," Ellie added. "We'll see you in the morning."

As soon as we walked away, Puppy started whining, yowling and scraping on the metal bars of the kennel. She was killing us! How could we leave her there like that?

Ellie and I looked at each other and knew what we needed to do.

We carried the kennel, with Puppy inside, out to the backyard and into the sukkah. She was going to join us for our sukkah sleep-out!

Dad, Jeremy, Ellie and I got all set up in the sukkah. The patio floor was cold and hard, so we layered a thick stack of blankets, one on top of another, before putting our sleeping bags down. We lined them up in a straight row with Jeremy all the way in the back against the wall, then me and then Ellie. Dad stayed by the doorway. We placed Puppy's kennel at Ellie's and my feet and put a few towels inside to cover her up and keep her warm. Then we draped a blanket on top of the kennel. She didn't complain, so we figured she was comfy. She was probably more comfortable than we were on the hard concrete floor and definitely more than she had been before we found her.

Lying down on my back, I looked up through the roof of cornstalks to see the night sky. The full moon was ridiculously bright—almost as bright as a car's headlights. I could see some stars twinkling but couldn't make out the constellations. I had looked it up earlier that week because I was curious about what I'd see, so I knew that the constellations of Pegasus and Aquarius were up there, but I couldn't see the full groupings through the s'chach. As I stared up at the sky, I thought back to what Rabbi Green had said in class. I imagined myself as an Israelite wandering in the desert, sleeping under the moon and stars, the very same moon and stars that I was looking at, in fact. Okay, well maybe not all the same stars because some may have imploded and some are probably new since three thousand years ago. But you get the idea.

Out of nowhere, a cold blast of air blew through the sukkah walls. I huddled under my sleeping bag and blankets. As I hid my head for warmth, I closed my eyes and my head began to race. I thought of that family I saw downtown earlier in the day. A swell of utter sadness washed over me. I realized that I was sleeping outside by choice but that there were people who were hungry and sleeping outside not by their own choosing. I thought of Mom sleeping cozily inside in her warm, comfy bed. I thought of the Israelites creating these makeshift shelters to keep them safe in the desert. I thought of Puppy who was so scared and lonely on her own. I could hear soft, contented breaths coming from inside of the kennel. *We all need shelter of some sort*, I thought sleepily as I rolled over and tried to make myself at home on the hard ground.

16

Corn Flecks and Dog Saliva

I brushed my hand across my face, wiping away whatever it was that was falling on it. This must have gone on for a while until I woke up with a jolt. I was all disoriented. Where was I? Why was I sleeping outside? Was it raining?

I rubbed my eyes and tried to get my bearings. I looked around. It was early morning. The sun was just barely coming out, making the sky slightly lighter so it was a little easier to see. Yes, I was in the sukkah. Okay, now it was starting to make sense. I looked around to see everyone else still sleeping, including Puppy who was in her kennel at my feet. I took a peek at my watch. It wasn't even six-thirty yet.

It was already starting to warm up outside, so I took off the sweatshirt that I had been sleeping in. I put my head down on my pillow and tried to fall back asleep. Then I felt it again. Something was falling on me. It wasn't rain. The sky was clear. I looked up just as I heard a scratching sound coming from the roof. Sure enough, there was a small squirrel up there eating the leftover corn from the corn stalks. It was holding a kernel in its paws and speedily chewing away. Now and then little pieces would fall down into the sukkah. I didn't like the idea of squirrel-saliva-covered-corn falling all over me, so I clapped my hands loudly once. It did the trick. The critter scurried away faster than a runner trying to make it to home plate on a pop fly. In an instant it was gone.

Luckily, I didn't wake any of the others with my loud clap. I fluffed up my pillow and squirmed into my sleeping bag, covering my head so that if the squirrel and some buddies were to return, I wouldn't get any more food falling on me. Finally, I drifted back off to sleep.

While I was sleeping, somehow my head found its way out of the sleeping bag. I became aware of this because I started to feel once again something dropping on my face. "Stupid squirrels," I muttered as I wiped away the stuff that was landing on me. This time, my hand felt wet. *Uh oh, it's raining*, I thought. I tried huddling under my sleeping bag but it was getting all wet.

Without opening my eyes, I sleepily groaned, "YaYa, Jay, Dad, get up. We've got to go inside. It's raining!"

No one answered. I finally opened my eyes and looked around. The sukkah was empty. Everyone—and everything—was gone. Sleeping bags, pillows, blankets, Puppy and her kennel, my family—all gone.

Why didn't they wake me up? I thought to myself angrily. *If they knew it was raining, why would they go inside and leave me out here?*

Then, as if the clouds were eggs that someone cracked open and let all the contents pour out at once, I felt a huge whoosh of water as it started to really come down. I got soaked. But something seemed fishy. I woke up enough to notice that the sun was out and shining as brightly as a summer's day in the desert.

"What's going on?" I grumbled out loud.

And then I heard them. My brother and sister were giggling from somewhere not too far away. I wasn't sure where their laughter was coming from, but I definitely heard them. They sounded like they were up above me.

I looked up at the house amidst the falling "raindrops" to see the two of them squirting me from the open window in my bedroom in the very same spot I had been with Ari and Jeremy a few nights ago, using the very same Super Soakers that we had used on Ellie and her friends.

"Cut it out!" I screamed.

Their giggles turned into full-fledged belly laughs. The "rain" stopped and they disappeared from the window above. I sat up and scrambled out of my sleeping bag. Small puddles were forming all over the ground around me, and the water had started to seep into the fabric of the sleeping bag.

"Oh, man," I said as I shook my head trying to get all the water out of my hair.

Before long, two figures eclipsed the light in the sukkah. I looked up to see my brother and sister hovering over me with the squirters in their hands.

"What'd you do that for?" I demanded.

"It's called payback," my sister replied calmly.

"Yeah, payback," Jeremy echoed.

"What are you talking about?" I asked.

"Um, I'm talking about the little rain shower that you and Ari created the night of my birthday party," Ellie said.

"I just like doing stuff to you," Jeremy added obnoxiously.

I looked directly at Ellie while wiping my neck with a dry part of my shirt. "What rain shower?" I asked, hoping that maybe I could still cover up and act innocent.

"You know," she said confidently.

Okay, I was busted. There was no denying it, so I confessed my guilt. "I thought *you* didn't know!"

"Of course I knew! Do you really think I'm that dense?"

"But you thanked me for not playing tricks on you," I said almost as a question.

"Well, sure. If I had told you then that I knew all about it, how could I have had my revenge like this? You'd be expecting something. This worked out beautifully," Ellie said with a huge smile stretched across her face.

"And I helped her because I wanted to. 'Cause I like doing stuff to you." Jeremy repeated.

"I can't believe you guys. Well, you really got me. I guess it had to happen sometime," I admitted. "But now we're even. Promise me that if we sleep out here again this week you won't squirt me anymore."

"I promise not to squirt you in the sukkah again," Ellie said.

I looked at Jeremy expectantly. He looked back at me blankly.

"Well?" I inquired.

"Well, what?" he asked back with his arms crossed against his chest, the Super Soaker hanging down at his side making him look like a soldier. Well, a soldier minus the buzz cut. And the uniform. And the disciplined, positive attitude.

"Promise you won't do this to me again!" I repeated.

"Fine. I promise," he gave in reluctantly.

As I thanked him, I caught a suspicious look between my two siblings. "Don't forget, you promised! No breaking promises!" I said. Hearing myself, I realized that I sounded nervous.

"Yeah, we know," Ellie said in a tone that wasn't all that comforting. "Anyway, it's time for you to get up. Mom told us we should wake you up. Guess our work here is done."

Just then I remembered Puppy. "Hey, did either of you take Puppy out for a walk this morning?"

"Actually, Mom walked her," Ellie answered. I could hear a hopeful tone in her voice. I knew exactly what she was thinking—the same thing that I was. Maybe Mom was growing attached to Puppy and would help us convince Dad that we should keep her.

Right then, as if she'd been waiting backstage to make an appearance on cue, Mom came into the backyard with Puppy on the leash. Puppy pulled away so hard that Mom dropped the handle of the leash and Puppy ran into the sukkah with it trailing behind her like an extra, bright red tail. She had definitely conquered her fear of being inside the sukkah. She jumped right on top of me and my sleeping bag and started licking my face. *What else is going to wind up on my face this morning?* I chuckled to myself. *Corn, water, and now dog saliva. What's the deal?*

Then I remembered that we were supposed to be careful around Puppy until her visit with the vet. "Oh no you don't," I said to her as I gently pulled her off of me, even though I loved that she loved me so much.

Meanwhile, Ellie and Jeremy quickly hid their water guns under my sleeping bag so Mom wouldn't see them.

"YoYo, I didn't realize you were up already. Did you take a shower?"

Ellie and Jeremy simultaneously hid their faces, both to hide their giggles and to avoid eye contact with Mom.

"You mean from Puppy licking me?" I joked. Then I answered for real, "Um, no." It would have been so easy to get those two in trouble but I decided to cover for them—this time. "I rinsed my hair because a squirrel was eating corn from the s'chach and it fell on my head." Well, that part was true anyway.

"Oh," Mom said. She bought it. "Anyway, are you guys coming to shul with us?" she asked.

I was now flat on my back with Puppy jumping happily all over me, wagging her tail wildly and switching back and forth between sniffing all over my body and licking my hands, arms, and face. "I think I want to stay home with Puppy," I said. "Is that okay with you?"

"I guess so," Mom replied. "I suppose someone should stay home and keep an eye on her. But I'd prefer that you not stay alone—"

Before Mom even got to finish her sentence, both Ellie and Jeremy shouted at once, "I'll stay home with them!"

"Are you both sure you don't want to join us? We only need one of you to stay home with YoYo and Puppy, the other can still come with us. Don't forget that today they'll have the Lulav Parade at shul."

"Oh, now I'm torn," Ellie lamented, "I *love* the Lulav Parade! I love walking around the sanctuary with our lulav and etrog and shaking them in all directions."

Another shocker.

"Mom, you don't have to call it the Lulav Parade anymore, we're eleven now, remember? You can call it

Hoshanot, its real name," I said. Actually, I still like doing the Hoshanot, but this year was a special situation.

"Wait, don't they do *Hallel* during services today, too?" Ellie asked.

"Yeah, today's a Hallel day," Mom replied.

"Oh, I love all the tunes in the Hallel service. Maybe I will go with you," Ellie said. "I never remember when we do Hallel and when we don't."

Mom answered, "It's always recited on the three Chagim as well as on Hanukkah and on Rosh Chodesh, the start of each Hebrew month. We say it at these special times to thank God for all the good things in our lives."

"Plus, they made it all sound so pretty. Yeah, okay," Ellie said, having made a decision. "I'll come with you guys. I really don't want to miss Hallel."

Then she looked directly at Puppy and wagged her finger right near her nose. "Don't learn any new tricks while I'm away, okay?" she said and ruffled the fur on the back of Puppy's neck. "That goes for you too," she quietly warned me with a little smile.

Mom turned to Jeremy and me. "Since the two of you will be here anyway, would you boys please bring the table back out to the sukkah and get everything set up for lunch? Grandma and Grandpa will be joining us, so please put out seven dairy place settings."

"Sure," I answered. "Assuming I can get away from Puppy for a few minutes," I said as she was crawling on my stomach. I was definitely falling in love with this dog. It was getting harder and harder to imagine wanting to find her owner. Looking around at everyone, I got the feeling that I wasn't alone in this. Puppy was certainly becoming part of the Silver clan. How could we possibly give her up?

17

A Whole Lot of Shaking Going On

Mom, Dad, Ellie, Grandma, and Grandpa returned from synagogue and joined us in the backyard.

"Thank you for helping out, boys," Mom said to Jeremy and me. "You did a fine job."

"Puppy helped, too!" I announced.

"Yeah, right!" Dad said, unconvinced, while raising one eyebrow. I love how he can do that. I try all the time, but I just end up looking like I'm really confused. Both Ellie and Jeremy can do it too. I wish I could but I don't think I inherited that gene. The only way I can do it is if I hold one eyebrow up and the other one down with my fingers.

"It's true," Jeremy chimed in. "She started chasing a squirrel at the other end of the yard, which gave us enough time to go into the garage and pull the table out."

"However, once she realized that the squirrel was almost as big as she was, she ran in the other direction," I said.

"It was pretty hysterical, actually," Jeremy concluded with a little chuckle. I liked that Jeremy was starting to care about and show some interest in Puppy. For a minute there, it felt like the old nice and fun Jeremy was back with us again. It seemed like a long time since he was his old self. I almost forgot that I once really liked being with him.

"But at least Puppy kept herself busy so that we could work," I added. "It was really challenging trying to get stuff done with her running around under our feet. We didn't want to step on her!"

Grandma said, "This sounds a little familiar. Deb, remember when YaYa and YoYo were babies? Wasn't it that way for you too?"

"Yes," Mom said. "I couldn't get anything done because as soon as one was content, the other one wanted my attention. I remember wishing that I were an octopus! I needed more arms, as well as more hours in the day."

"Speaking of more hours in the day," Grandpa said, "I'm hungry. Time's a wastin'. Let's eat!"

We all gathered around the table. Dad recited Kiddush and when he was done he asked, "Who would like to be the first one to say the blessings over the lulav and etrog?"

"I'll do it! I'll do it!" Ellie volunteered. "I love doing the *brachot* for Sukkot! I love *everything* about this holiday, even saying the brachot!"

I felt like I was having déjà vu. I could have sworn that I'd already lived through this whole scene once before. Very recently.

"Here you go," Dad said, handing her the lulav and etrog.

In her left hand, Ellie took the long palm branch with myrtle leaves sticking out of it on one side and willow leaves on the opposite side, held together by a woven handle. Then she took the lemon-like etrog in her right hand and started to recite the blessings. Mom interrupted just as she started to say "*Baruch...*"

"Turn it over, YaYa. The *pitom* faces down when you say the *bracha*," Mom instructed.

"Oh yeah, I forgot. It's been a whole year, after all!"

Ellie followed Mom's instructions and turned the etrog over so that the pitom, the little woody stem at the top of the fruit, faced the ground. She started over but once again she was interrupted, this time by Grandpa, right as she said, "*Baruch atah...*"

"Wait, wait," he said. "You need to face east toward Jerusalem!"

"Oh yeah!" we all said together, laughing at ourselves. It's not like we'd never done this before.

We all made a ninety-degree turn so we were facing the back of the sukkah, which was east. We knew that because there was a big sign that said "*mizrach,*" which means "east," on the back wall.

She started up once again. This time she got as far as "*Baruch atah Adonai...*" when Jeremy called, "Time out! You have your hands switched. You need to hold the lulav in your right hand and the etrog in your left. We just talked about that in shul school."

This was getting to be quite comical. Ellie switched hands and looked around at everybody. "Sheesh! Anyone else want to chime in? Now's your chance!"

We all laughed.

"I think you're good now," I said.

"Okay, I'm facing east, the pitom is down, I've got the lulav in my right hand and the etrog in the left. Good?"

"Good," we all cheered.

"Okay then, here we go," she said. "*Baruch atah Adonai, eloheinu melekh ha'olam asher kid'shanu b'mitzvotav v'tzivanu leishev ba'sukkah.* Blessed are you, Adonai, our God, Ruler of the universe, who has sanctified us with your commandments and who has commanded us to dwell in the sukkah."

Ellie looked very proud of herself as she went to hand back the lulav and etrog to Dad.

"Hold on," Dad said. "You still have one more to do. You just said the blessing for dwelling in the sukkah, now you need to do the second one for the lulav and the etrog."

"Duh! I'm such an airhead today," Ellie said. Then she recited the second blessing: "*Baruch atah Adonai, eloheinu melekh ha'olam asher kid'shanu b'mitzvotav v'tzivanu al n'tilat lulav.* Blessed are you, Adonai, our God, Ruler of the universe, who has sanctified us with your commandments and who has commanded us concerning the waving of the lulav."

Ellie once again went to hand back the lulav and etrog.

"You're in a hurry to get rid of that stuff, aren't you?" Dad laughed. "You're still forgetting one more thing. You need to shake the lulav and etrog together."

"How could I forget?" Ellie said. "I guess I'm just so excited that it's finally Sukkot that I keep getting flustered."

"Don't forget to turn the pitom back over again," Grandpa instructed.

"Got it," Ellie said.

And just as Rabbi Green had done in class the other day, Ellie shook the lulav and etrog in all directions: up, down, left, right, forward and backward. She did not, however, stand up on top of the table to do it. I don't think that would have gone over too well with our parents.

"Do you know why we shake the lulav in all directions?" Grandpa asked.

"To remind us that God is everywhere," Ellie answered.

"Good girl!" Grandpa said proudly.

Pep-rally Ellie finally got to shake her pom-poms. Well, not exactly pom-poms, but she finally got to shake something!

When she was done, we all took turns holding the lulav and etrog, shaking them and saying the blessings. Then, after all the ritual stuff before the meal, we finally got to sit down and eat. Mom and Ellie served their amazing squash soup. After the soup course, we enjoyed Dad's delicious "secret recipe" salmon, an incredible casserole with rice and roasted vegetables and who-knows-what-else.

I'm not a huge fan of vegetables in general, but I really did enjoy the ones we had in the sukkah. We have a rule in our house that we have to, at the very least, try whatever is being served. Every now and then I actually do like something that I was expecting to find disgusting. Like spinach kugel, for example. It sounds absolutely gross, but one time my Mom made it and I had to try it. I took the smallest, pea-sized piece that I could possibly pick up on my fork and ate the required sample. To my huge surprise, it wasn't only tolerable, it was great! Now I actually request spinach kugel all the time.

After we finished our lunch, Grandma carried out a glass baking dish that she held using a dishtowel. In the dish was the apple crisp that she had made and brought over. As she placed it on a trivet in the middle of the table, I could smell the sweet, tart aroma. I thought about how much I loved fall foods like squash soup and apple crisp. I don't know if the food really was better than usual, or if it was because we were eating in the sukkah, but everything tasted extra-good. Most of all, I was happy to be enjoying a great meal with my family, and in particular, my family that included a new furry member, even if it was only for the time being.

18

Puppy Love

Dad carried out a big urn of hot water. I took a mug and a tea bag and made myself a piping hot cup of lemon tea. It wasn't cold out, but I love drinking tea when I eat Grandma's apple crisp. It's my own personal tradition. I could see the steam come out of the mixture in the baking dish as she scooped each serving. I couldn't wait for mine!

As we began eating the delicious dessert, Ellie said, "We need to name the dog. We can't keep calling her Puppy."

"But Ellie," said Mom, "just as I said in the car yesterday, the problem with giving her a name is that it will make us feel even more like she's ours, and until we are certain that someone isn't looking for her, I feel very uncomfortable doing that."

"Plus it might confuse her if she already has a name that her owner gave her," Dad added.

"Well, how about this as a compromise," I offered. "We won't call her by the name we come up with until we're sure that we can really keep her but we'll refer to her by that name when we're talking *about* her, just not directly to her."

"I guess that does deal with the issue of confusing her, but I'm still concerned about growing too attached to her if we have to give her back," Mom said.

"I'd really like to give her a name," I replied, "even if it might make things harder later on. I feel so weird calling her Puppy all the time. Everyone should have a name. I mean, it's not like you go around calling me 'Boy,' right?"

"I could think of worse things to call you," Jeremy noted in his predictable tone.

"I agree that Puppy deserves a real name," Ellie said. "It almost feels rude."

"Same here," Jeremy agreed.

"Well, I suppose we could give her a name for when we're talking about her amongst ourselves," Mom conceded. "What do you think, Mark?" she asked, turning to Dad.

"Sure, let's see what we come up with. Our family's good at coming up with nicknames," he said, winking at me.

Jeremy got us rolling. "Since we found her in October, why don't we call her something like Octodog."

"Octodog?" Both Ellie and I questioned together.

"That's the dumbest name I've ever heard!" Ellie laughed out loud.

"All right Freak Face, what's your brilliant idea?" Jeremy asked in a harsh tone. Mom shot Jeremy one of her famous "stop it now" looks. I guess he had forgotten about losing his phone but once he realized what he had just said he seemed to also realize that he would lose his phone and possibly more for even longer. He quickly corrected himself. "What's your idea, YaYa?" He asked, his voice oozing sweetness and yet somehow simultaneously delivered a hidden mocking tone. Mom didn't pick up on it, but we sure did.

Ellie ignored his sassy tone. "I don't know. But I kind of like your idea of naming her based on when we found her. How about if we call her Autumn?"

"And you thought Octodog was dumb?" Jeremy snorted. "Next!"

"Leafy?" I threw in.

"No!" all six of my family members proclaimed at once. I didn't realize that Grandma and Grandpa were going to be a part of this decision but I guess they felt pretty strongly about that suggestion.

"Pumpkin?" I tried again.

"Ooh, that's a possibility!" Ellie said.

"It's better than Leafy," Jeremy snarled.

"Haystack? Cornstalk?" I rattled off.

"Hey, wait. I have an idea," Mom said, "Since she's staying with us for Sukkot, how about if we give her a name based on the holiday?"

"Like what, Mom? Sukkie? Etrog?" Jeremy muttered. "I don't think so."

Ellie jumped up and yelled out, "S'CHACH! We should name her S'chach!"

"You've got to be kidding!" Jeremy howled. As much as I hate to admit it, I absolutely agreed with him.

"That's way too hard to pronounce, sweetie," Dad said. "Can you imagine calling, 'Here S'chach'?" Dad asked. "And just think about how other people would have trouble saying it. They'd call her Scratch, Skak, anything but her real name. Let's keep going."

And then I got it. It hit me all of a sudden and I knew at that moment, that I had come up with the perfect name for our—well, not yet our—family dog.

"Lulav!" I called out. "LuLu for short. She'll have a cute little nickname like the rest of us."

"Oh, I love it!" Ellie exclaimed.

"Little LuLu. I love it too," Mom said.

"I can live with that," Jeremy added.

"Nice one!" Dad said, patting me on the back. "So we all agree? Her name, at least when we're talking about her, will be Lulav, LuLu for short."

That was fun. But at the same time it was sort of sad. We were naming her, and even with the compromise, we all knew in our hearts that with every passing moment we were getting more and more attached to her.

We finished our meal and just as we were about to clear our dishes, we heard the gate to our backyard squeak as it swung open. Then there was a knock at the entrance to our sukkah. We had a surprise guest.

19

Lost and Found

I'm sorry to interrupt," Rabbi Green said, poking his head through the doorway, looking a bit awkward. "Chag sameach, everyone."

"Come in, Rabbi," Dad said, "what a wonderful surprise." He and Grandpa got up to shake hands with him as he entered the sukkah.

LuLu's tail started wagging like crazy and she ran over to Rabbi Green, jumping from her hind legs. She put her front paws up on his pants leg. He bent down to pet her and she went wild. She must have remembered how well he took care of her when we found her in the sukkah at shul yesterday. I guess it really is true that dogs have a strong sense of smell. She must have recognized his scent and maybe his voice too.

"Well, will you look at her!" he beamed. "She looks like a completely different dog from the one we met yesterday."

"We're having a great time with her here," I said. "She's been the best Sukkot guest we've ever had, and we have a lot of Sukkot guests."

"Rabbi Green, guess what!" Ellie exclaimed excitedly, racing toward him and practically pouncing on him the way LuLu did. "We gave her a name! Guess what we named her. You'll never guess!" And without giving him even a moment to take a breath let alone to answer she spouted, "We named her Lulav because we found her in the sukkah and she came home with us on Sukkot. Her nickname is LuLu! It was Joel's idea."

"That's cute," he said, but he didn't seem nearly as enthusiastic about it as I expected him to be. In fact, I was pretty disappointed by his reaction. I thought it was a really creative name.

"Would you like some lunch? We just finished but we have plenty more," Dad offered.

"Oh no, thank you," he began. "I'm actually on my way home to my own sukkah for lunch. I told Rebecca that I was going to be a bit late but I'm sure by now she's wondering what happened to me."

Rabbi Green, his wife Rebecca, and their kids live only a few blocks from us. Our house is between Ohav Zedek and the Greens' house, so they pass by us all the time when they walk to and from synagogue. "I have something I want to share with you and I waited to come by, hoping that by now you'd be done eating." A look of importance washed over his face. He clearly had something he needed to say. I didn't like the expression he was wearing.

"What's going on?" Mom asked. "Is everything okay?"

"Yes, well, um, I'm not even sure how to begin," Rabbi Green said as he stopped petting LuLu and stood up straight again. "I guess in one way the news I have is really good news but I'm afraid you kids might not see it that way."

We all looked at him expectantly. I had a very bad feeling about this.

"Okay," he began. "Well, as I was walking home a little while ago, I happened to notice a piece of paper lying on the ground upside down. I assume that it had been posted on the utility pole on the corner of 35th and Walnut and fell off. I bent down to pick it up and when I turned it over...." He removed the folded piece of paper from his pants pocket, opened it up, and shook it out.

My eyes began to sting as if I had been working in a chemistry lab without goggles. He held up a flyer with the word "LOST" in giant red letters on top and right underneath was a picture of LuLu. I felt sick. I felt like the ground was going to come out from under me. I felt like I wanted to run up to my room, curl up into a little ball, and cry my eyes out. I felt like I wanted to grab LuLu and run away with her. The flyer meant that she belonged to someone else. And they were looking for her. And that she would never be a part of our family.

Ellie did start to cry. My mom's eyes got wet and teary too. Even Jeremy looked like someone had knocked the wind out of him.

I stood up and asked Rabbi Green for the paper. I didn't want to cry, but I couldn't help it. I held the sheet of paper in my trembling hand and some of my own teardrops fell onto the page, which then rolled off the paper and dripped onto the ground. The paper read, "LOST: One year old female dog named Daisy. She has run away and we are worried sick about her. Please contact us with any information. Mary and Henry Browning." Below their names was their phone number.

The atmosphere in the sukkah changed dramatically from happy and joyful to one of intense sadness.

"When I first saw the sign, I was so excited to know that the lost dog had a home and that her owners were looking for her. Knowing that she has been in your loving care I could imagine how thrilled the owners would be. But, as I also feared, it appears that you have grown attached to her in a very short time. Saying goodbye will be very hard, I know." He looked at each of us with an expression that said, "I'm so sorry."

I stood there holding the paper in my shaking hand, when all of a sudden I brightened. "But look! It says that the dog is a year old. LuLu is just a puppy! This can't be her!" I knew in my heart, looking down at the picture, that this probably wasn't true but I was clinging to the possibility.

"Yeah," Ellie agreed, "LuLu's just a puppy. This isn't her!"

Rabbi Green said, "I thought that for a moment, too, but take a look at this picture. The dog in the photo has the exact same brown markings around her eyes and the little white spot by her nose. We assumed she was a puppy because of her size, but I guess she's just a very small dog." This time he actually said out loud, "I'm so sorry."

"It's true," Mom said. "She didn't have even a single accident since she's been with us. I didn't really think about it at the time but she was definitely trained to go outside. A puppy would never know where and when to go to the bathroom."

She had a good point there.

I had another glimmer of hope. "We can test out her name! If she answers to Daisy, then we'll know that for sure it's her, but if she doesn't...."

"We can try," Dad said with a doubtful tone in his voice.

I went out of the sukkah and called, "Daisy, come here Daisy!" She didn't move. She was busy sniffing around under the table looking for crumbs and scraps of food dropped during lunch.

Ellie and I looked at each other through the sukkah doorway and smiled.

"Let me try," Ellie said as she joined me outside the sukkah. "Here, Daisy! Here, girl!"

Again, no response.

"You see, I don't think it's the same dog!" I said excitedly as Ellie and I went back into the sukkah.

"I don't know," Rabbi Green said. "It sure looks like the dog in this picture."

"So, what should we do now?" Ellie asked.

Rabbi Green said, "I actually know the Brownings. They live a few blocks from me and I bump into them every now and then at the bank or the grocery store. I didn't even know they had a dog, let alone that they lost one. But I would be happy to stop at their house on my way home and let them know that 'Daisy' may have been found."

"How about if you take us there and we'll bring *LuLu*," I said, emphasizing her proper name, "and they can let us know if she's their dog or not."

"*Not*," Ellie whispered under her breath.

Grandma said, "I think that's a great idea."

Rabbi Green agreed. "However, since I'm already so late for lunch, how about if you come over to my house around two-thirty. We'll go to the Brownings' together and I'll introduce you. In the meantime, you can enjoy your time with Dais—," he cut himself off, "—LuLu until then."

"Sounds like a plan," Mom said.

"Okay, see you soon," Rabbi Green said and left our yard.

Ellie, out of habit, looked down at her bare wrist to check the time. "This is going to be the longest stretch of time ever," she grumbled.

And she was right. It felt like the longest hour and a half of our lives. It was worse than being in the doctor's office waiting room when you know you're going to get a shot. Worse than sitting through never-ending previews before the movie you've been waiting all year to see begins. Worse than waiting for the snow to melt so the baseball field is usable again.

Yep, all we could do was wait. We tried to keep ourselves busy. We helped clean up after the meal. We walked Grandma and Grandpa to the door and said goodbye. We played in the yard with LuLu, passing the time until we could go meet the Brownings, and hopefully prove that we didn't have their dog.

20

A Daisy By Any Other Name

Mom, Dad, Jeremy, Ellie, and I positioned ourselves behind Rabbi Green as he knocked gently on the Brownings' dark red door. We were all quiet. The only sound we could hear was the soft tinkling of the metal wind chimes dangling over the porch. A wooden plaque on the door said, "Welcome," and even though their front porch felt very cozy, with two rocking glider chairs and some hanging plants, I didn't feel very welcome. I felt like I wanted to get out of there as quickly as possible...with LuLu in my arms.

"Who is it?" a shaky, old voice came from the other side of the door.

"It's your neighbor, Jonathan Green," Rabbi Green said. We never call him by his first name, and even if we did, we would do what most people do, which is call him by his Hebrew name, Yoni. It sounded so weird to hear him say that. I didn't see a mezuzah hanging on the doorpost so I guessed that this family probably wasn't Jewish and might be more familiar with the name Jonathan than Yoni. I figured that was why he used his English name.

We heard the click, click of the lock opening from inside the house, and a tiny woman peeked her head out from behind the door. She smiled politely at Rabbi Green and the wrinkles next to her eyes grew a little deeper when she did.

"Hello, Jonathan! What a pleasant surprise!" Then she looked at the rest of us and ran her hand across her short silvery-white hair, "Oh my goodness! It's a party. If I had known I was going to have company, I'd have gotten dolled up!" Then she delicately covered her mouth and giggled like a little girl.

"I hope we're not coming at a bad time," Rabbi Green said.

"Oh no, dear, not at all. Who do you have with you here?"

Rabbi Green motioned to us with his outstretched arm. "These are my friends the Silvers. They live a few blocks north of here." Ellie stood one step below me in such a way that Mrs. Browning couldn't see her or who she was holding in her arms.

"Nice to meet you. Would you like to come in? Maybe have a cup of tea?" She seemed quite excited to have some company even if we were strangers. It was also clear that she hadn't seen LuLu (or Daisy) yet by her very matter-of-fact attitude.

"Sure, thank you," Rabbi Green led us in as Mrs. Browning held the door open for us, stood back, and called, "Henry, we have company! Come down here, please!"

The minute we stepped over the threshold, LuLu went berserk. She wriggled out of my sister's arms and hopped down to the carpeted floor, barking, wagging her tail and jumping up and down all at once.

"Daisy!" Mrs. Browning exclaimed with such excitement that she reminded me of a kid winning tickets to the World Series. For seats behind home plate. For the final game.

The dog jumped all over her legs.

"Down, girl! Down!" she cried. "Yes, I'm happy to see you too, but don't hurt Mama!" Ouch, that stung.

I was heartbroken. It seemed that this was, in fact, Daisy the missing dog. I know I should have felt good seeing how happy the two of them were to be reunited but I didn't. I was devastated by the thought of losing LuLu. I did wonder why she didn't answer to the name Daisy when I called to her in the sukkah but she definitely seemed to be at home here. *She must be their dog*, I admitted to myself reluctantly.

"Daisy girl! Where've you been?" A cheery, older man joined us in the entryway. He leaned over and LuLu jumped all over him, licking his hand and running circles around his slippered feet.

Rabbi Green introduced us all one by one to the Brownings.

"Please come in and have a seat," Mrs. Browning said as she shuffled over to a big armchair in the living room. She motioned for us to find a seat on one of the sofas. The dog jumped right into her lap.

"Oof," she gasped.

"Well," Rabbi Green began, "I guess you can figure out why we're here."

"This is so wonderful!" Mrs. Browning said, wiping tears of joy from her crinkled eyes. "Where on earth did you find her? We were worried sick about her."

"Believe it or not," Rabbi Green said, "we found her inside the courtyard of our synagogue. We are currently celebrating a holiday called Sukkot. One of the things we do on the holiday is build temporary structures in which we eat and gather over the course of the holiday. The sukkah, which is like a hut, is not particularly useful as a sturdy sort of shelter but I guess it provides slightly more protection than living on the street.

Somehow, she found her way into the sukkah within the courtyard and cozied up behind a bale of hay and some cornstalks. How long had she been missing?"

"Almost a week now," Mr. Browning answered. "We were afraid we'd never see her again. We couldn't imagine she'd be able to survive out there on her own. This is not the first time she's run away but it is the first time she's been gone for this long. We had just given her a bath and we had taken off her collar, which is why she didn't have any identification on her. She's made running away a bit of a habit, but she always managed to find her way back to us until now. We were about to give up hope."

Mrs. Browning added, "Our children suggested that we do some sort of 'chipping' procedure after the last time she ran away, but I didn't like the sound of it and frankly, we never did quite catch on to that new-fangled stuff."

"Yeah, I heard of that," Jeremy said. "It's when they inject a microchip right under the animal's skin so they can scan a lost animal and find the owner by a GPS satellite. I just read about that online not too long ago. It's pretty cool."

"Well, I guess we're a bit out of date with all the new technology," Mrs. Browning said. "Our children said that they would take her in to 'get chipped,' as they put it, the next time they were in town since we had no idea what they were talking about. But Daisy ran away before they came for their next visit. Meanwhile, we really do need to do something. She is a sweet, lovable dog but she doesn't listen to us very well. She's not very obedient. Sometimes she doesn't even answer when we call her."

"That explains why she didn't come when we called her by name either," Ellie said.

Then Mrs. Browning turned to me, Ellie, and Jeremy, as we sat together on the couch. "So you children brought her home and took care of her?"

"Yes," we all answered together. Actually, Ellie and Jeremy said "yes." I just nodded because I really couldn't speak at all. I felt like I had a lump the size of a tennis ball inside my throat.

"I cannot thank you enough!" she said, blowing her delicate, wrinkled nose into a tissue. "We love our sweet little Daisy, don't we, dear?" she said, turning to her husband.

"Yeah, she's a cute one, that Daisy. But, awfully frisky! Sometimes I wonder if we made a mistake adopting her at our age. Our kids gave her to us as a gift because they thought it would be nice for us to have a dog to keep us company. But we can't seem to keep up with her. I do worry about her safety all the time," Mr. Browning said. I noticed that his hand that was resting on his lap was shaking a whole lot. It didn't seem to be shaking the way my hand did when I was holding the paper earlier. That was due to nerves. I think he was shaking due to old age.

"It is a lot of work taking care of a dog," Mom agreed. "They do take a lot out of you, almost like infants."

I mustered up the strength and the courage to speak. My voice was a bit shaky but I managed to say, "Maybe we could come over and help you take care of her. We've really grown to like her in the short time that she came to stay with us."

"We could come over and walk her," Ellie offered.

"And we won't charge too much, either," my brother added.

"We won't charge *anything*," I jumped in. "We just want to visit with Lu—Daisy," I said.

"That's a lovely idea," Mrs. Browning replied. "That's one of the hardest parts for us. We can't take her for long walks. Sometimes she gets so excited when she sees other dogs that she tugs on her leash. I worry that I'm going to fall. And now with winter approaching, I'm afraid of slipping on the ice on the sidewalks."

"It almost happened a couple of times to each of us last year," Mr. Browning added. "That would have been a disaster. It's not only her safety that we worry about but our own as well."

"I would be happy to have you come over and walk her. And you can come and visit her anytime you'd like, even if she doesn't need to be walked," Mrs. Browning said. "It would be wonderful to have some young people in our home now and again. Now that our children have all grown up and moved away, we see them so rarely."

Mr. Browning added, "I would be happy to pay you for your services."

"No, no," Ellie said, "Seeing Lu—Daisy would be payment enough!"

"Well, how about a plate of cookies waiting for you?" Mrs. Browning asked.

"Deal!" I said, smiling politely. I knew it was the right thing to do but inside my stomach I felt like there was a boxing match going on. Even though it would be great to see LuLu, and it sounded like we could see her every day if we wanted, it wouldn't be the same as having her live with us as part of our family.

We stayed at the Brownings' for a while. The grown-ups sat in the living room and chatted while the three of us kids took LuLu out to the backyard and played with her. We threw sticks for her to fetch and ran all around the yard with her chasing us. It was so much fun that for a short time I even forgot that she wasn't going to come home with us.

But then it came time to leave and we had to say goodbye to LuLu. That tennis ball-lump reappeared in my throat. I bent down and hugged her and she licked my face all over as if my head were a huge lollipop. It was probably one of the hardest things I've ever had to do, leaving her there. I knew she was happy to be with the Brownings but I also knew that she had been happy with us.

We walked home empty-handed and in silence. No one was yanking and pulling us from the other end of the leash or stopping along the way to sniff every inch of pavement. It was the most miserable walk of my life.

Who Can It Be Now?

My Dad, Ellie, and Jeremy went to synagogue again the next day but I wasn't feeling well. I stayed home and moped in my bed for most of the morning. Mom stayed home to take care of me. She brought me a hot-pad to keep on my stomach. I felt tired and kind of like I was rocking on a boat that was going over ten-foot waves. Mostly, though, I just felt sad. I couldn't explain it either. I mean, we only had LuLu with us for a little over one day but despite my parents' warnings, I did fall for her—hard. I knew from the get-go that we might not be able to keep her but I was hoping against all odds that it might still work out. I never imagined that we would actually find loving owners who missed her.

I felt a little better after Mom brought me some oatmeal on a bed tray. That's one thing I do like about being sick at home. I love to eat in bed. When I finished the oatmeal, Mom took the tray back down to the kitchen and I sat and read in bed.

By the time the others came home I was feeling a lot better, especially when I kept myself busy and kept my mind off of losing LuLu. Mom came in to my room and checked my forehead. "Well, YoYo, the good news is that you seem to be fever-free. Do you think you're feeling well enough to join us in the sukkah for lunch?

I have some chicken soup with matzah balls. That might help you feel better."

"Yeah, chicken soup with matzah balls sounds really good right now," I said, gently swinging my feet over the side of the bed and slowly getting up. I put on a pair of sweatpants and a t-shirt and went downstairs to join my family.

We did all the sukkah stuff again: the blessings, shaking the lulav and etrog, and eating together. As I sat there and sipped spoonfuls of Mom's delicious soup, I was painfully aware that no one was sniffing around and rubbing up against my legs under the table.

The sliding glass door between the patio and the house was open and just the screen door was closed to keep the bugs out. From inside the sukkah, we heard the doorbell ring in the house. We all looked at each other, confused.

"Were any of you expecting anyone?" Dad asked.

"No," we all answered.

"Maybe it's a package," Ellie suggested brightly.

"It's probably someone selling something," my brother said.

"I'll go and see." Dad got up from the table and scooted out of the sukkah. I heard him slide open the screen door then I heard it slide shut.

I could hear Dad talking to someone at the front door. It was muffled and I kind of tuned it out, focusing on the delicious food in front of me. Just as I was dipping challah in my second bowl of soup I heard the screen door slide open again. From inside the sukkah I could now clearly hear Dad talking to someone. I looked up and saw him standing at the entrance to the sukkah with someone behind him. And then I heard those familiar yips!

Before I knew it, LuLu was inside the sukkah, jumping excitedly from each one of us to the next one. She didn't know where to start.

"LULU!" I cried out, not remembering (or caring, really) that her "real" name was Daisy. I had even forgotten that we weren't going to call her by that name directly. It just felt so right.

"LuLu?" Mrs. Browning questioned.

"Sorry, I meant Daisy," I said quietly. I was embarrassed that I had called her that in front of them. I guess it's not really nice to rename someone else's dog and ignore the name they gave her.

"LuLu is a cute name," Mrs. Browning said. "I rather like it. It makes no difference really, she doesn't answer to the name we gave her anyway. May as well call her what you want!" She chuckled, shaking her head. "Such a silly girl!"

"Well, please come in," Mom said to the Brownings. "Welcome to our sukkah."

"This is the holiday shelter that Rabbi Green was telling you about at your house yesterday," Dad said to Mr. and Mrs. Browning as they looked around appreciatively.

"This is lovely," Mrs. Browning said, looking at the gourds and the decorations hanging from above. "It's so festive!"

"Joel and I were going to come visit you later on today and take Daisy for a walk," Ellie said, stumbling over her name. "We miss her already."

"Yes, well, that's actually why we've come over. We wanted to talk with you about the arrangement that we had offered you yesterday," Mr. Browning said.

A feeling of dread and worry flushed over me. Were they going to tell us that we couldn't come and visit LuLu after all? Or were they going to insist that they pay us to walk her and make it an official job? That would be okay, I supposed, but then it might end up feeling more like a chore than a treat.

Mr. Browning sat down and said, "After you left yesterday, Mary and I started talking. For some time now, we've been thinking of selling our home and moving into a smaller senior-living apartment. We've been looking at a place a few towns over."

I gasped. This was worse than I thought. Did they come over to tell us that they were going to take LuLu away from us? I was starting to feel nauseous all over again.

"We love our little Daisy like one of our own children," Mr. Browning continued. "She keeps us company, adds life and spunk to our home, and cheers us up when we're feeling a bit down."

"However," Mrs. Browning continued where he left off, "as we mentioned yesterday, we are having a hard time keeping up with her. She is so full of life and energy and we simply can't play with her the way she would like us to."

They were confusing me. I wished they would just get to the point already.

"In addition," she said, "as Henry mentioned, we are thinking of getting a place over at Park Square Senior Apartments. We've had our eye on one particular unit for some time now."

Ellie gasped. I didn't understand what was going on. Was she thinking the same thing that I was?

Mrs. Browning went on. "Park Square is absolutely perfect for us in every way, except for one."

"They don't allow pets," Mom said knowingly.

"Well, they do allow cats and other pets that stay in the apartment, but they don't allow dogs."

"Yes, I remember visiting that building and I had heard about that. I took part in an art show in the lobby there once. I think that's a fairly common policy in many senior buildings. What would you do with Daisy?" Mom asked.

"Well, dear, that is exactly the problem. If we were to move to Park Square, we could get a cat or a tank full of fish, but we could not take Daisy along with us. So Henry and I got to talking yesterday after you all left our home. It's quite clear to us that you and Daisy, or LuLu, if you wish, have taken quite a liking to one another."

Now it was my turn to gasp. I felt my eyes bugging out as I looked at Ellie. She was sitting there motionless, with her hand over her mouth. I glanced at Mom. She had tears welling up in her eyes.

Mr. Browning continued, "We were wondering if you might want to take our sweet Daisy into your home."

"You mean, if you should move, right?" Mom asked, I assumed for our benefit, making sure we all understood exactly what they were saying.

"Actually, we were thinking that she might be better off with a lovely young family such as yours right now. We simply can't keep up with her," Mrs. Browning said.

"You want to give her to us?" Jeremy blurted out. Mr. Browning nodded

"For keeps?" Ellie cried. Mr. Browning nodded again.

"No way!" I shouted.

"No?" Mr. Browning looked confused. "But I thought for sure...."

"No, I mean yes!" I jumped in. "I meant no way, I can't believe it!"

Ellie unclasped her hand long enough to say, "Oh my goodness!"

"No way!" I repeated.

"Oh my goodness!" Ellie repeated.

"Are you serious?" Jeremy chimed in.

"Wow!" Mom couldn't hold back her excitement. In fact, I think she may have been even more excited than the rest of us.

"Are you sure about this?" Dad asked.

"Well, yes, but it's under one condition," Mrs. Browning said. "We would love it if you would bring Daisy or LuLu to visit us now and then. For now, we'll still be in our house up the street but it would be wonderful if you would come and visit us with her at Park Square if and when we do move. Of course, she wouldn't be able to come upstairs but we could meet you at the park right outside the building."

"We realize that we're springing this on you out of the blue and we're not expecting you to decide right at this moment," Mr. Browning said. "Think about it and get back to us. But if you are not going to be able to take her in please let us know as soon as possible because we will start contacting people right away to find her a home. We've made up our minds about this. Giving her a good home would be best for everyone."

"Can we keep her? Please?" Ellie and I sang out together. Jeremy looked pleadingly at our parents but didn't say anything.

Our parents looked at one another. It felt like an eternity until Mom finally spoke, "I know we all were kind of secretly hoping for this moment but now that it's here we really need to think this through. While having a dog would be tons of fun, there are other things we need to consider."

"Yeah," said Dad, "like vet bills and food, and of course it's a time commitment. I think we need to talk about it before we make a decision."

"Can she at least stay with us for the afternoon while we talk about it?" I asked.

"Sure," the Brownings said together. "If it's okay with your parents," Mrs. Browning added looking at Mom and Dad.

"That would be fine," Mom said, as if it was even a question with her.

"Sure," Dad agreed.

Mrs. Browning knelt down and patted LuLu on the head. "Be a good girl, Daisy dear," she said as if talking to a child. "You have nice behavior for our new friends, you hear?" And with that, the Brownings thanked us for welcoming them into our sukkah and they headed out. Mom and Dad walked them to the front door. The minute they returned we all started in on our parents at once with our voices joining as if one chorus:

"Can we please keep her?"

"They can't give her to someone else!"

"We love her so much! She's already part of our family!"

"PLEASE!"

"We've always wanted a dog."

This went on for a few minutes. Finally, we stopped badgering them and we all got quiet, waiting for a reaction.

Dad said, "I'm just not sure. I agree that Lulu is a sweet, lovable dog. She's done a good job of making her way into all our hearts. But it's a lot of work taking care of a dog. Deb, do you think it's a good idea?"

"You know, I realize that this sort of came out of nowhere, and we're not all that prepared to take in a dog, but to tell you the truth, I do. I almost feel as if the kids finding the lost dog was sort of *bashert*, like it was meant to be. And we've always said that we would get a pet for the kids someday," she replied. *They did*? I had no idea!

"And the dead crab I brought home from the beach when I was five doesn't count," Jeremy said.

"Neither does the class gerbil that I 'babysat' over winter break when I was in second grade," Ellie added. "Especially since all it did was sleep all day. What fun is that? Now, LuLu on the other hand, she's a *real* pet."

Clearly, Mom was into the whole idea. We just needed to convince Dad. I picked LuLu up and held her in front of my face, so that she was eye level with him. I spoke in a high voice so that it would seem like LuLu was talking. "Please let me stay with you, Mr. Silver. I promise to have good behavior. And I won't chew up any of your shoes. And I'll sleep in my kennel if you want me to. And I'll always obey your commands. And I'll do tricks for you. I'll roll over, speak, and even play dead. Just please don't send me away. I love the Silver family!"

Once again it was quiet in the sukkah, aside from the leaves on the roof rustling and an airplane flying overhead in the large clouds.

"Here's why I'm concerned, kids," Dad started abruptly. "Believe me, I wish I could say that I would help take care of her too. But I have late hours at the store two nights a week and when I get home I'm tired. And forget about the winter holiday season. I'm never around then, as you know. Your mom is busy working at home and can't be bothered by someone who needs her attention all day long while you're at school."

This wasn't going the way I had hoped.

"It won't be any trouble for me as long as we train her to stay out of my belongings," Mom said. It was so cool that she was with us on this. Usually Mom and Dad are a strong, unbreakable team. It was sort of weird to hear them be on different sides of an issue.

"Really?" he did his one-eyebrow thing again.

"Really," Mom said. "It might be nice to have someone keeping me company while I'm working in the studio. It gets kind of lonely here during the day."

"We'll take care of her, Dad, don't you worry. We promise," I offered.

"Please think about it!" Ellie begged.

"Okay."

I glanced over at Ellie, and through our twin non-verbal communication, raised my eyebrows to indicate, "Great! He's going to think about it!"

She gave me a secret thumbs-up under the table.

"I said 'Okay'," Dad repeated, this time a lot louder.

We all looked at him. "Yeah, we heard you. Thanks for thinking about it," Ellie said.

"So?" Dad asked.

"What do you mean, so?" I asked.

"What do you mean what do I mean? I mean okay. Okay! All right! Yes, let's keep her! Let's add a four-legged member to the family!" he finally said with a huge grin.

"AAAAAAHHHHHHHH!!!!" We screamed so loud-ly that I was sure the neighbors would come running or call the police. Or that we caused an airplane to go off course. Or the International Space Station.

Ellie bent down and swooped LuLu into her arms and danced around with her in the minimal space in the sukkah. "LuLu Silver!" she sang. "Welcome to the family! I can't believe it! This is even better than you guys promising to take us to Splash World!" Ellie said to our parents without taking her eyes off of LuLu.

Mom went over and hugged Dad. "I'm glad we're on the same page about this one, honey," she said while giving him a squeeze. "I think this is going to be great for our family."

This was turning out to be the best Sukkot ever!

22

Want Some Fries with that Shake?

A couple of nights later, it was really warm out during the day and Ellie and I decided that we wanted to sleep in the sukkah again. We had to beg Mom and Dad to let us do it because we had school in the morning but we promised that we'd wake up and get ready on our own. We even brought out two battery-powered alarm clocks so we would be sure not to oversleep. I figured that this would further prove our ability to be responsible.

Dad asked if we'd be okay out there without him because his back was bothering him from sleeping on the ground the other night. We thought about it for a minute and agreed that we'd be fine out there on our own.

Jeremy warned us that the weather report said that it was going to be cold overnight, so he opted to sleep inside as well. In the end it was just me and my sister. I was relieved that my siblings weren't going to be out there together because I didn't like those shifty looks they were giving each other after they sprayed me with water the other morning. At least I got them to promise that they wouldn't do that again.

As far as LuLu was concerned, Dr. Donohue came to take a look at her and said that she looked good and healthy. As it turned out, LuLu was already a patient at her veterinary clinic so Dr. Donohue already had Lu-Lu's records under the name of Daisy Browning. She was up to date with her shots but needed a new collar with her new name. We also set up an appointment to get her a microchip so that if she decided to run away again we'd be able to find her easily.

After Dr. Donohue's thorough examination, she announced that LuLu was free of ticks and fleas (yay!) and could stay in the house without posing a problem for us. Mom suggested that she stay inside for a while because she needed to get used to sleeping in our home. She had been sleeping outside for so long, Mom was worried that she might have trouble being in the house now and she wanted to train her.

Ellie and I got set up on the ground next to one another. We slid into our sleeping bags and lay on our backs, looking up at the sky through the s'chach.

"This has been an exciting Sukkot, huh?" she started the conversation.

"I don't think we'll ever forget this one," I agreed.

"Who would have thought that what started out as a regular, normal day at Hebrew school—"

"Regular and normal?" I interrupted. "Do you remember seeing Rabbi Green shaking like a milkshake on top of his desk? That's normal?"

"It is for Rabbi Green!" Ellie answered. "Ha! Shaking like a milkshake! That's funny!"

"I was going to ask him if he wanted 'some fries with that shake,' but I didn't know if he'd get my sense of humor, so I decided not to make any smart aleck remarks," I said.

"I bet he'd think it was funny," Ellie said confidently. "He's pretty cool. Now, if you'd asked him if he wanted a burger with that shake, he might have been offended."

"Well, duh! That's not kosher. That would be mixing milk and meat."

"Exactly."

"Well, if I know Rabbi Green, and I believe that I do, he'll be back on top of his desk again soon, shaking what his mama gave him for some other reason," I said. "Like maybe for Hanukkah or something."

"No way, goofball!" Ellie exclaimed. "He'll spin for Hanukkah! Like a dreidel." We both laughed.

"Good point. Well, maybe for Tu B'shvat, when he's shaking like a date tree. Or on Purim, when he's shaking a *grogger!*"

"Or on Passover, when he's shaking all the matzah crumbs off of his pants!" Ellie said, laughing so hard she was gasping for breath.

At this point, in Jeremy speak, we were both practically ROTFL at this hilarious conversation. Then, catching us off guard, a big, cold gust of wind blew through the sukkah as if a giant were standing on the other side huffing and puffing. We stopped laughing at once, taken aback by the bone-chilling blast, and huddled up inside our sleeping bags. Brr! All of a sudden it was so cold!

"This weather is crazy," I said. "One minute it's so nice and warm and the next it's like sleeping on a polar ice cap."

"It definitely adds to the challenge," Ellie agreed. "I heard that it's supposed to warm up a bit overnight and actually be fairly warm in the morning."

"I hope so," I said as I shivered and once again thought about the family that I saw on our way to the farmers' market.

"Hey, Ellie," I said.

"Yeah?"

"Remember that family I told you I saw the other day when we were going downtown?"

"Uh huh."

"Where do you think they are right now?"

"I have no idea. What do you think?" she asked sliding deeper into her sleeping bag, snuggling in to hide from the artic breezes that were now continually attacking us.

"I was just thinking about them. I wonder if they have a home. I wonder what their story is. The sign the kid was holding up said they were hungry. I wonder if they're sleeping outside like LuLu was before she found her home with us."

"What made you think of them now?" Ellie asked.

"Actually, I've been thinking about them a lot since I saw them. I can't stop. I feel so bad. Just now I started to feel cold and I'm wondering if they're out there freezing. Winter's going to be here soon and it's only going to get worse."

"Yeah, I know what you mean," she replied. "It's really sad."

"I guess we could try to do something to help them," I suggested.

"Like what?"

"I don't know, maybe bring them some food or something?" I said. "Remember how hungry we were during Yom Kippur? And we only fasted until the afternoon. Can you imagine how it must feel to be that hungry and not know if or when you're going to get food again?"

"Ooh, I like the idea of bringing them some food," Ellie said excitedly, sitting up, still wrapped in her sleeping bag, looking like a human burrito.

"Maybe we should think bigger," I said. "After all, just because we saw one family that needed help, it doesn't mean there aren't other people who are cold and hungry. Maybe we can do something to help even more people. You know, we each got a bunch of birthday money. Maybe we can take some of our cash and buy food and give it to a shelter."

"Yeah, and maybe we can try to organize something at school to get even more people to pitch in," Ellie suggested. "Or we could try to do it at the synagogue."

"Hey! I'm having a brainstorm!" I popped up too, also looking like a loosely wrapped burrito. (Or perhaps an eggroll, a blintz, or a crêpe.) "The next time we'll have a large gathering at shul will be on *Simchat Torah*, with everyone coming to celebrate and dance with the Torahs. Maybe we can try to organize a food drive then. I know there's a food collection box by the synagogue office, but people don't always remember to bring donations. We can do a big campaign in time for Simchat Torah."

"That's in less than a week. Do you think we can organize a project like this so quickly?" Ellie asked.

"Yeah, I don't think it will be such a big deal. We'll email everyone we know, and we can put up flyers all over the synagogue. All we have to do is ask everyone to bring at least one item with them, like a can of food or something, when they come to celebrate Simchat Torah. It's perfect," I said. "It could even be something they already have in their cupboards. They won't even need to go out and buy anything. I really think this could work."

"We should talk to Rabbi Green and see if maybe he could help us get an email out to the whole congregation," Ellie remarked. "I really like this idea."

"Me, too. I think this could be great," I replied, getting really excited.

"You know, YoYo," Ellie said, "you had said that you don't love Sukkot as much as I do because it leads right into winter. Maybe, in addition to food, we could also organize a coat drive because that would help people without a lot of money to stay warm. It will make you feel good to do something positive and it will turn the one part of Sukkot that you don't love so much into a part that will make you feel better."

"YaYa, that's really nice. The thought of having a coat drive is making me feel better already," I managed to vocalize during a huge yawn. "Hey, I'm getting pretty tired. Let's sleep on it for now, and tomorrow we'll talk to Mom and Dad and Rabbi Green."

"Okay," Ellie agreed. "I'm getting a kind of sleepy too. And I'm kind of cold." She rolled over and snuggled back into her sleeping bag. I could only see a few strands of her hair sticking out of the opening of the bag.

"Can you breathe in there?" I asked.

"Mhmm."

"Okay then. Good night."

I could barely hear her muffled response coming from within the sleeping bag.

"Gdnt."

23

A Time to Cry and a Time to Laugh

In the morning, the birds starting chirping, singing, and communicating back and forth, and it woke me up before my alarm clock went off. I was conscious enough to realize that I wasn't getting sprayed with water by my siblings. It was a peaceful, quiet, nice way to get up. It was also much warmer than it had been at night. This weather was so weird! I heard the occasional rumble of cars driving down our street. The world was beginning to stir so I figured it was time for me to do the same. But when I looked down at the alarm clock, I realized that I didn't need to get up just yet and could get a little more shut-eye. In fact, I had a lot of time before I needed to get up. I rolled over again, enjoying the extra time before I had to wake up and get ready for school.

I fell back asleep but at some point I felt something tickling my face. *Oh no, not again! They promised!* I thought to myself, starting to get annoyed. *They'd better not be squirting me!*

I opened my eyes and looked around. No water. No squirrels or corn pieces either. Must have been a fly or a mosquito or something, I thought. I looked over at the mound that was Ellie in her sleeping bag. I couldn't believe she slept all night tucked up like that. Then again, Ellie's always been a really good sleeper. She usually wakes up with just barely enough time to gulp down some breakfast and run to the school bus in the morning. Amazingly, she hasn't missed the bus yet this year. Some days it's really close but Roy, our bus driver, hasn't had to leave her behind. Yet.

I closed my eyes for a moment or two, when I felt the pesky mosquito on my cheek again. I went to smack it, which only served to make me hit myself in the face. *Not smart!* I thought. Then I was pretty sure I heard someone chuckle but I was really confused because I didn't feel any water and I didn't see anything suspicious. I looked over and saw the big lump of Ellie wrapped inside her sleeping bag.

When I was fairly confident that I was just being paranoid and that nothing was going on, I closed my eyes again. Not long after that, I felt another tickle on my face. I opened my eyes and saw something that made me scream like I was on a thirty-story rollercoaster. Right there, sitting on my sleeping bag, looking me in the eye was the biggest, hairiest raccoon I ever saw in my life!

"AAAAGH" I screamed, squirming backward out of the sleeping bag and racing out of the sukkah.

Then I remembered that my sister was still in there. I knocked on the thin, wooden walls, and called, "Ellie! Wake up! Get out of there right now! There's a raccoon in the sukkah!"

I ran back around to the doorway to see her. She didn't move. Not even a twitch.

"ELLIE!" I bellowed. How could she not hear me? How could she be so sound asleep? And how could I save her from the raccoon?

I was just about to dash inside to get help from my parents when I saw something that made my stomach do flips. I saw my brother and sister hiding behind the wall on the other side of the sukkah, doubled over in hysterics. Ellie had tears flowing down her face and Jeremy was gasping for air. They actually were, quite literally, rolling on the floor (well, the ground) laughing. *What the heck?*

I looked inside the sukkah and saw a huge, stuffed toy raccoon lying on its back with its fake-furry legs pointing upward to the sky. I must have kicked it when I jumped out of the sleeping bag and it landed upside down on the sukkah floor. I observed the lifeless lump in the sleeping bag and noticed a pillow corner and a part of a blanket sticking out from the top. Ellie wasn't even in there! They got me again. I couldn't believe it!

I walked around to where they were. "Hey! I thought you weren't going to play any more tricks on me!" I shouted at them as they sat on the grass high-fiving one another and laughing so hard that there was no sound coming out of their mouths.

When she finally caught her breath enough to speak, Ellie said ever-so-cheerfully, between gasps, "Good morning!" Then, to add insult to injury, she pulled out a camera and snapped a picture of me in my pajamas.

"Good morning? What do you mean 'good morning'? You scared me half to death! And you broke your promise! You weren't going to play tricks on me anymore!"

"Oh no, we did not," Ellie said in a victorious tone. "We promised not to squirt you in the sukkah. And we didn't. We never said anything about waking you up with a stuffed raccoon!"

"Heh heh," Jeremy snickered like an evil villain as he high-fived Ellie again.

"And why are you taking pictures of me?"

"Oh, I don't know," Ellie said coyly, "why did you take pictures of me and my friends the other night?" *She knew that too?*

"You guys stink!" I shouted, starting to feel a lump in my throat like I did the other day when I thought we were losing LuLu. I did not want to cry in front of them but I was mad, embarrassed, and upset that they made me their victim once again.

"YoYo, you've been playing tricks on us for years. It's about time you got some payback," Ellie said defensively. Then I think she saw how upset I was because she came over and put her arm around me. "Why are you so sad?"

"I don't know. I'm not used to being the one who gets tricks played on them. I guess I can dish it but I can't take it."

Ellie unzipped the camera case and slid the camera back inside. It seemed to me that she was done pranking me, and that maybe she was even starting to feel bad. *Good!* I thought. "Well, we were just fooling around. We certainly didn't mean to make you sad," she said.

"Yeah, I'm actually okay with it," Jeremy said with his usual obnoxious flair and a shrug of his shoulders.

I made a face at him as if to say, "Get out of here, jerk." Of course I didn't actually say it out loud because if I had, he would undoubtedly have tackled me, hurt me, and somehow managed to get *me* in trouble with Mom and Dad. Instead, I turned and headed toward the house without saying another word. Remember when I said, "Older brothers...who can understand them?" What I think I meant to say was "*My* older brother...I *can't stand* him!"

Ellie followed me, stopped me by grabbing onto my shirt, and turned me around.

"YoYo, listen," she said. "I'm really sorry. We were just kidding around and I didn't think you'd react like this. I wasn't trying to upset you. I thought you'd laugh about the whole thing."

I could tell from the sound of her voice that she really did mean it. My brother, on the other hand, was already gone, back inside the house not feeling the slightest bit of regret.

"You know," Ellie continued, "I have been your number-one target since the very first time you put a whoopee cushion on my seat at Thanksgiving dinner when we were four, and I've never felt sad about it. Embarrassed? Annoyed? Angry? You know it! But I'm not sure I get this whole being sad thing. Maybe you should try to remember how this feels the next time you want to play one of your tricks on me, or anyone else for that matter."

She was starting to sound like Mom. She was right, I knew, and if she hadn't been dressed in Corey McDonald pajamas, with her hair in pigtails, I might have thought that she was a forty-something adult trying to teach me a life lesson.

"Okay, fine. And you promise me that you won't play any more tricks on me?"

"Will you promise the same thing back?" Ellie asked. *When did she get so good at making bargains?* I wondered. She must have learned a thing or two from Dad, the king of making deals.

"I guess," I responded half-heartedly. I've always enjoyed pulling pranks on her. What would I do for fun now?

Just then, Ellie pulled out the Super Soaker and pointed it at me.

"You *just* said that you're done pulling pranks on me!" I said sounding much whinier than I meant to.

"I'm not pulling a prank on you. I'm starting a water fight with you!"

"You also promised you wouldn't spray me anymore. Don't your promises mean anything?"

A deeper voice came from behind me. "We promised that we wouldn't spray you in the sukkah anymore. You're not in the sukkah. Time for your morning shower," Jeremy said.

I was now fairly convinced that both of my siblings were going to grow up to become politicians because they were so very careful with their wording and made sure that their "promises" worked for them. Talk about reading the fine print!

I knew what I had to do. I sprinted to the back wall of the garage so fast they didn't have time to hit me. I picked up the water hose, turned it on full blast and aimed the nozzle directly at Jeremy. I took all of my anger and frustration out on him. It felt so good! Once he was as thoroughly soaked as a noodle in a pasta pot, I smoothly swooped across to Ellie. It was the biggest water fight we'd ever had. Ellie started to scream and wound up with a mouth full of water. We were all trying not to laugh but it wasn't easy because the whole scene was so funny. Never, in all my years, had I woken up on a school day to a water fight. It was really something!

Mom came out to the backyard wearing her bathrobe and holding LuLu in her arms. *Oh no! She's gonna kill us!* I thought. Actually, I think we all thought the same thing at the same time. I ran to turn the hose off and dropped the nozzle on the ground next to me. Jeremy and Ellie dropped their squirters too. All three of us stood there dripping from head to toe. We looked like we had all gone swimming with our pajamas on.

I could feel my face get hot. It felt like all the blood in my body rushed from way down in my toes all the way up to the top of my head. I knew that my entire face was turning tomato-red and that my freckles were probably completely hidden.

Mom stared at us, open-mouthed, while LuLu's tail wagged furiously. She wriggled in Mom's arms, trying desperately to jump down.

"I cannot believe you guys!" Mom started.

Ellie shot me a look as if to say, "Here it comes...." I could tell that she felt the same *Uh-oh-we're-busted* feeling as me because, sure enough, her ears transformed from pink to bright red.

I decided to nip this in the bud. "I'm sorry, Mom."

"Yeah, me too," Ellie joined in.

"We all are," Jeremy said. I don't think any of us actually believed him, but at least he was smart enough to know what to say and when.

"Well, you should be!" Mom scolded. "I can't believe you did this!"

Dad came out to see what was going on, wearing the matching bathrobe to Mom's. Bubby and Zayde bought them "his and hers" bathrobes for their anniversary last year.

"Holy moly!" Dad said and whistled as he looked around. This was getting worse and worse by the minute.

"We're really sorry!" Ellie and I said at the same time.

"Can you believe these kids of ours?" Mom said to Dad.

"No. No, I cannot," he replied, shaking his head in deep disappointment.

That lump started forming in my throat again as Mom continued.

"I can't believe that they asked—no—begged for a dog. Then, they go and have a water fight, and have a ton of fun and leave LuLu out! And what about us? What do they think we are, chopped liver?"

What? I heard the words coming out of her mouth but they just weren't making any sense to me. I was sure that I didn't hear her right.

Mom put LuLu down on the ground and yelled, "Go get 'em, girl!" LuLu went wild. She didn't know where to run first. She jumped on each one of our legs and then splashed in the puddles we created in the lawn. Meanwhile, as if they'd rehearsed it for months, Mom and Dad whipped their bathrobes off, displaying their bathing suits.

"You think we don't have windows upstairs?" Mom asked. "Remember how at Rosh Hashanah we promised we'd lighten up this year and have some fun with you? Well, look out, because here comes some fun!"

We kids were dumbfounded, frozen, in a state of shock. None of us could move. This worked out well for Mom and Dad because Mom snatched the Super Soaker from the grass behind Ellie while Dad made a beeline for the spigot and turned the knob. In one fell swoop he grabbed the hose from the ground by my feet. The two of them went to town, flooding us mercilessly, not that it mattered because we were already drenched. Jeremy, Ellie, and I just stood there taking it because we couldn't believe this was really happening! Parents...who can understand them?

"By the way," Dad shouted over the rush of water coming from the hose, "we finally picked a date to take you guys to Splash World. We're going in two weeks. This is your warm-up!"

LuLu jumped and played under the falling drops of water, splashing and shaking the water off of her fur, only to get wet again a moment later. She barked happily, enjoying the silliness.

Once the shock wore off, we three made a run for it, giggling and tripping along the way. It was both fun and bizarre seeing our parents being so childish and goofy.

"Into the sukkah!" Jeremy called to us. "They won't spray us in there. The sleeping bags are inside." We bolted into the shelter of our temporary home and indeed, our parents did not spray us in there. It was a great plan except for when LuLu followed us. Her wet paws were covered with grass clippings and mud. She jumped all over us, the sleeping bags, the pillows and even the stuffed raccoon. In fact, when she spotted the furry toy, she leaped right on top of it and started wrestling with it. She chewed on its fuzzy neck and dragged it around in her teeth. It was a pretty funny sight given that the fake raccoon was almost twice her size.

From inside the sukkah, we heard a third voice in the backyard, a man's voice. I was curious to see who was out there but was pretty embarrassed about the way I looked. I was sure that Ellie and Jeremy felt the same way. Jeremy peeked through a knothole in the wood wall of the sukkah.

"Who is it?" Ellie asked quietly.

"I can't see from here," he answered, moving around in all directions trying to get a view of the uninvited guest.

All at once, as if she smelled doggy pot roast or something, LuLu tore out of the sukkah and started doing her famous yips. I couldn't stand the suspense and decided that I didn't care what I looked like. I stepped out of the sukkah and into the bright sunlight. Ellie and Jeremy followed.

24

Pride and Joy

I should have guessed. It was Rabbi Green. No wonder LuLu ran out of there so fast! She was trying to jump up on him in all her mud, grass and raccoon-fluff glory. He, on the other hand, dressed in neat khaki pants and shiny brown loafers, backed away.

Lulu was such a huge mess. I hoped he wouldn't think that we weren't taking good care of her. Then again, we were all a mess! We looked like a family of castaways that had recently jumped ship and swam ashore. Well, Mom and Dad looked semi-okay because they were back in their bathrobes, which I'm assuming they threw on quickly upon hearing Rabbi Green enter our yard. It became clear within a moment that Rabbi Green was not concerned about any of this.

"*Boker tov*, Silver kids!" he cheerily greeted us as if nothing was strange or unusual, as if every family he visited early in the morning was sopping wet, filthy, and wide awake. On a school day!

"Boker tov," Ellie said back. "Good morning!"

"Morning," Jeremy mumbled, looking down at the blades of grass between his toes, clearly embarrassed to be seen like this.

"*Boker or*," I answered, remembering that sometimes you can respond to someone wishing you a "good morning" in Hebrew with that reply, which means "morning light."

"I was just on my way to morning *minyan*," Rabbi Green began. I could see my parents squirming a bit because they rarely go to synagogue for *shacharit*—the morning prayer service. Dad in particular looked as guilty as if he had just been caught shoplifting.

"Don't worry, Mark, I don't judge," the rabbi said with a friendly wink, as if reading Dad's mind. "And believe me, if we needed a tenth person to help us make a minyan, I wouldn't hesitate to call." Everyone knows that my Dad doesn't have a far commute in the mornings like a lot of other parents because The Silver Lining bookstore is less than a mile away. Sometimes Dad even walks to work when the weather's nice and he doesn't have to schlep a lot of things to the store. Mom's commute is the easiest of all because it simply consists of climbing two flights of stairs to the attic.

Rabbi Green continued. "Normally, I would never stop over this early in the morning but it sounded very lively back here, so I figured you were out and about and that it would be okay to stop and ask how things were going with the dog. I heard the big news from the Brownings."

"Oh, everything's great!" Mom chirped. "She is just the sweetest little thing. We should have called to tell you the news ourselves but it's been so hectic around here, thanks in no small part to this new family member we've adopted."

"No need to apologize. I certainly understand," Rabbi Green said, smiling. "I'm thrilled to hear that it all worked out. I don't want to be in the way. I just thought I'd stop and check in but I'd better get going before they start without me."

"Wait, Rabbi, since you're here, Ellie and I have a question for you," I said.

Ellie and I told him all about the family I saw and about our idea for the food and coat drive. He looked at us as though he might burst with pride. Then he looked at my parents and gave them an approving look. "You folks are clearly doing something right! I'm almost even a bit jealous of little LuLu here because she gets to be a Silver. Such a nice family!"

"That's very sweet of you, Rabbi," Mom said, blushing slightly.

"You know, we've sort of had a chance to experience what it's like to not have a real roof over our heads by eating and sleeping in the sukkah this week," I said. "For us, it was a lot of fun. But we also realize that for LuLu and maybe for some people, it's not all fun and joyful. We chose to sleep outside but if it would have gotten too cold or rainy, we could have gone inside."

"Not only could you go inside, but did you know that if it's too cold or rainy you're supposed to go inside? When it is no longer enjoyable, you are no longer performing the mitzvah of dwelling in the sukkah. Remember we talked about the names of the holiday? One name is Z'man Simchateinu, the time of our great joy. The Rabbis taught that if staying in the sukkah becomes a hardship, then it is not only permissible but preferable to stay indoors," he said.

"But that only works if you have a place indoors to go," I said.

"Precisely," Rabbi Green agreed. "I will absolutely help you with your food and coat drive. After all, in the morning prayers that I'm on my way to say, we praise God who 'clothes the naked,' malbish arumim. And how does this happen for those who have no clothing?

Through acts of kindness such as yours. It would be my honor to help you to help others."

"There's a morning prayer about clothing people? That's cool. So, is there also one about feeding the hungry?" I asked.

"Well, there are two prayers that might refer to feeding the hungry indirectly. One is 'HaNotein LaY-aeif Koach,' which means, God who gives strength to the weak. One way of gaining strength is by eating. Just look at what a difference some food did for little LuLu," Rabbi Green said, looking at LuLu, whose tail was wagging as fast as a hummingbird's wings. "The other one that could be related to food is 'She'asah Li Kol Tzorki.' This one thanks God for giving us all that we need. Obviously food is a very basic need. As is shelter, as you kids have discovered."

"I didn't even know that you guys were thinking of doing this," Mom said. I noticed that her eyes looked a little damp and I was pretty sure it wasn't from the water fight. She gets a bit emotional sometimes.

"We just came up with the idea last night," Ellie responded. "It's kind of hard to believe, since it's so warm out now, but it got pretty chilly in the sukkah and we started talking about people who might be sleeping outside who were probably cold and hungry."

Mom turned to us and said, "I'm so proud of you!" And she kissed each one of us on top of our heads. Even Jeremy.

Ellie and I glanced at each other, and I knew that she was thinking the same thing that I was: *And what exactly was it that Jeremy did lately that made her proud?* But we didn't say anything.

"You should be proud," Rabbi Green remarked, "and you guys should feel great about what you're doing! *Kol hakavod*—way to go!" He looked down at his watch. "Well, I'd better be off," he said, heading for the gate. "I'm really going to be late now. But it was worth it!" he said, grinning at the two of us. "Let's talk later on today about the details of your project?"

"Sure," Ellie and I said together.

"Sounds great," he said. "See you later!" and with that, he jogged out of our yard.

"You know, I need to do some more 'mitzvah stuff' for my bar mitzvah," Jeremy said making air quotes. "Maybe I can get some 'mitzvah points' if I help you guys with your project."

"You know, you could even help us just for the sake of helping out," I responded harshly. I found his statement to be quite annoying but decided to focus on his offer to help and not on his reason. "Sure, you can help us," I said in a softer tone.

After all the excitement and activity of the morning, we suddenly realized it was almost time to catch our bus. Ellie and I ran upstairs to get ready for school. We took turns taking super speedy showers then raced to our rooms to get dressed. From behind my closed door and hers I heard a huge, loud muffled scream.

"YaYa, you okay?" I called out.

"I FOUND IT!" I heard her shout.

"Found what?" I called back while hopping up and down, doing the ancient dance known as putting on your socks while standing up.

"My watch! It was in my underwear drawer!"

Of course it was. Isn't that where everyone keeps their watches? I thought to myself.

Ellie and I rushed downstairs, each grabbed a piece of toast with jam that Mom had left for us on the kitchen counter, and ran to the front door where we grabbed our backpacks. For the first time, I felt like I was my sister, who has mornings like this all the time. It was most out of the ordinary for me and rather unsettling. Ellie was used to it. Like racehorses heading for the finish line, we were off.

25

Dancing With the Cars

On Erev Simchat Torah, before services began, Ellie and I lugged three huge empty boxes into the front entryway of the synagogue. Ellie had covered them with wrapping paper to make them look nice. Jeremy carried in the big poster board sign we had made and placed it on the easel that the custodian had left out for us. The sign had large red, eye-catching glittery letters that read, "Food and Coat Drive Here!" Ellie wrote and decorated the words. I cut out pictures of cans of food and winter coats and put them all over the sign. Jeremy ate some carrots while he watched us work on it. (Just kidding!) In all fairness, he actually did help us a lot by making flyers on the computer to hang up in the synagogue. We really managed to pull it all together.

We weren't sure what to do because we were so excited about our project and kind of wanted to stand around to see if the boxes would get filled up but we also wanted to go in and celebrate Simchat Torah. Ultimately we decided that the sign was in a good location and people would figure out what to do with their stuff if they brought any, so we went in to join the festivities.

It was amazing how different the atmosphere was in synagogue on Simchat Torah compared to Yom Kippur when everyone was tired and hungry and the mood was intense and serious. On Simchat Torah it was fun and festive and wild!

Simchat Torah is when we celebrate the end and restarting of the Torah-reading cycle. I always feel a sense of accomplishment during this holiday. There's something very satisfying about finishing and starting all over again from the very beginning. Every week at shul, we read a portion of the Torah. Bit by bit, over the course of the year, we get through all five books of Moses. So Simchat Torah is like a big, giant, crazy party celebrating that we made it through the whole thing.

When it was time for the *Hakafot*, the time when everyone danced with the Torah scrolls, we all held hands and made circles, dancing around the people who were holding the Torahs. Some of the grown-ups had little kids bouncing around on their shoulders. A group of women made their own circle and were doing Israeli dances. Everyone was singing, clapping, and smiling. And with the way the Torah scrolls were being carried and lifted in the air, it almost looked like they were dancing too!

I've never been to a Jewish wedding before, but from what I hear, people dance in circles just like at Simchat Torah, but instead of the Torahs being the center of attention, it's the bride and groom. I got a quick, burst of excitement right then for Aunt Rachel and Uncle David's upcoming wedding. If dancing with the Torahs was this much fun, then I figured dancing with people on one of the happiest days of their lives must be as much fun if not more!

For the final hakafah, Rabbi Green led everyone outside to the parking lot. Luckily, it was a nice, warm night, unlike the night we almost turned into popsicles in the sukkah. As we danced through the entryway, past the donation boxes, I took a quick peek to see if anyone had brought anything in. I counted about six or seven coats and jackets piled up in the coat box and about a dozen or so cans of food. Not great, but at least it was a start.

We danced with Rabbi Green in the lead, singing (almost screaming, really), skipping, and generally making a lot of happy noise. It was so much fun being with the whole congregation, dancing and celebrating. We were loud, but not too loud that the neighbors would complain. Clearly we were "happy in our festival," as the sign in the sukkah had read.

After a long session of dancing in a circle, Rabbi Green formed a sort of conga line and we all followed him, laughing, giggling, and goofing around. It was one thing when it was all of us kids doing that with him in class the other day. It was a very different thing to see all of the adults being silly and goofy right along with us, kind of like how our parents were during our water fight. And in all of our silliness, we followed the rabbi between and around the parked cars. The parking lot was full and fairly dark and so it was a bit of a challenge to dance our way around out there. But we managed and had a great time doing it.

After dancing, spinning, waving little flags on sticks, singing, clapping and finally running out of breath, we made our way back inside. I checked again, and not surprisingly, I didn't see any change in the contents of the boxes.

We returned to the sanctuary to finish the Torah service. Members of the congregation went up and took turns reading Torah aloud. My parents and grandparents were given the honor of going up for an *aliyah* to recite the blessings before and after a section of the Torah was read.

At the end of the readings, Mr. Pinsky, one of the congregants, was given the honor of *Hagbah*—lifting the Torah. He held on to the wooden handles at the bottom of the scroll and carefully slid the Torah to the end of the lectern, squatted down and lifted the Torah way up high for all of us to see the words inside. The Torah is written on a long piece of parchment and rolled up onto two sticks with handles. Because we had gotten to the very end, the two halves of the scroll were completely lopsided. One side was basically empty and the other side was heavy with all of the parchment rolled up on it. Every year on Simchat Torah, I hold my breath, worrying that the person doing Hagbah is going to drop the Torah, but luckily I've never seen that happen. Mr. Pinsky came through for us again this year.

After the whole service was done and we were getting ready to leave, Rabbi Green came up to Jeremy, Ellie, and me and said, "Silver kids, I'm really proud of you and your efforts to help people in need. It looks like a few people got your message and have started to help."

Ellie looked a bit discouraged, "Yeah, but only a few. This isn't going to help too many people."

Rabbi Green put his hand lightly on her shoulder and said, "Yael, at least six people will be warmer now simply because you thought enough to reach out to them. And a few people will be a bit less hungry as well."

Ellie shrugged and said, "Yeah, I guess so." I have to admit, I felt the same way.

Rabbi Green continued. "You know yeladim, this doesn't have to be a one-night only event. How about if we continue to post about this in our synagogue bulletin and keep these beautiful boxes that you made for a couple of months? We didn't give people much time to respond, so maybe if they get a reminder or two, we'll get even better results."

I liked that idea and so did Ellie. I decided to lighten the mood with one of my little jokes. "Yeah, let's see if we CAN make a difference!" I said while pointing at the cans in the box. "Get it? 'Can'?" I'm not sure but I think even Rabbi Green, the most good-humored and patient guy in the world rolled his eyes at me. Apparently it wasn't one of my better puns!

My family walked home on the dark sidewalks together. I could still hear the tunes from the hakafot in my head and Ellie sang and twirled under every streetlight.

We made it home, and the minute the key turned in the lock of the front door, LuLu began barking from inside the house. I had had so much fun at synagogue but as soon as I heard her little yippy "voice," I couldn't wait even one more second to see her and play with her. Ellie had a look on her face that I read to mean that she felt exactly the same way.

The instant we got inside, Ellie and I ran to the kitchen to open up LuLu's kennel and let her out. We were in such a hurry that we bumped into each other as if we were in an old black and white Three Stooges movie. We opened the kennel and LuLu made a mad dash out of there. She barked happily under our feet and started yipping and leaping around our legs. She even started running around in circles, chasing her own tail. Then she started doing everything all at once, leaping, barking, and chasing her tail until finally she plopped on the floor, worn out from her burst of energy. But that tail of hers kept thumping on the wooden floor making a fast drumbeat. With her long, pink tongue hanging out of her mouth, she panted and watched us, waiting to see what was going to happen next.

"Hi, LuLu!" I exclaimed, not sure which one of us was more excited at that moment. I was so busy having fun that evening that I didn't realize how much I missed her. It's hard to say goodbye to her each day when we have to leave for school, but at the same time, it's also so great knowing that she'll be here waiting for us when we get home.

"Hello, Miss LuLu," Ellie said as well.

LuLu jumped up and down and in circles again. It reminded me of how we were jumping around and going in circles not too long ago with the Torahs. But somehow I don't think it would work out too well for LuLu to dance with a Torah! Before long she started sprinting up and down the stairs, back and forth, up and down. Every time she came back to the kitchen she checked in with us and stopped long enough to lick each of our hands before bolting back up the stairs for another round of rowdy-dog laps.

Dogs...who can understand them?

Ellie and I smiled at one another. This felt so right. LuLu sure seemed happy.

And at home.

Acknowledgments

There is no way that I could have brought YaYa and YoYo to life on my own. I want to extend my gratitude to everyone who has helped me in one way or another, from confirming the accuracy of information to proofreading, critiquing, and sharing opinions. I so appreciate all that you've done to help me with this book.

To my wonderful husband Gary: Once again, I want to thank you for all of your patience, guidance, and feedback. I love you so much and am so glad to be on this journey with you.

To Ari, Ilana and Eitan: You probably barely remember a time when YaYa and YoYo weren't a part of our family. Thank you so much for listening, suggesting, and helping me shape the characters in this book. You may recognize some of their characteristics or situations. Our family gives us lots of good material to work with! I love you guys with all my heart.

To Leslie Martin, my editor extraordinaire: Thank you so much for all of your patience with me as I constantly put new changes in front of you. You have such a great eye and are so careful with each and every detail. I also love when you push me to change things that don't feel right to you. Ultimately, even though I may push back, it seems to always turn out that you are right!

To Ann Koffsky: Thank you so much for your amazingly vibrant and fun cover art. I love it! It truly captures the essence of *YaYa & YoYo*.

To the Bettenhausen crew: Thank you sharing your

family's raccoon adventures. (I told you I'd work a raccoon into the story!)

To Lisa Simon: Thank you so much for batting clean-up and doing the final proofreading. Your suggestions were perfect.

To the kids who helped me at the Heilicher Minneapolis Jewish Day School: Thank you for your guidance about which vocabulary words were too hard or just right. And to all the kids who read the manuscript and shared feedback, thoughts, and opinions: Thank you all so much. Your advice and input made a huge difference.

To my friends and fans on Facebook and other online and offline locations: Thank you so much for answering my questions and responding to my informal questionnaires. I really do listen to everything you have to say. And thanks so much for all of your kind words and support. It means the world to me!

Special thanks to Rabbi Alexander Davis, Rabbi Avi Olitzky, and Rabbi Kerry Olitzky for your Judaic input and fact-checking. In addition, aside from asking questions or using information that I already have learned over the course of my lifetime, I did refer to one book for many answers: *The Jewish Holidays*, by Rabbi Michael Strassfeld. New York, Harper & Row Publishers, 1985. (An updated version of this book was published by HarperCollins in 1993.)

And of course, thanks to all of the *YaYa & YoYo* fans out there. These books are for you. I'm working on Book 3 now!

About the Author

Dori Weinstein is an award-winning author who grew up in Queens, New York. Her first book in the *YaYa & YoYo* series, *Sliding Into the New Year*, won a Moonbeam Children's Book Award gold medal. Dori is a graduate of Binghamton University and Teachers College, Columbia University. She taught in public schools in New York City as well as at the Talmud Torah Day School in St. Paul, Minnesota. She currently teaches Hebrew to preschoolers. Dori lives in Minneapolis with her husband Gary and their three children (but thanks to allergies, no pets other than a ceramic dog named Cicero).

Visit Dori on Facebook, Twitter, and on her website at www.yayayoyo.com.

29680355R00118

Made in the USA
Lexington, KY
03 February 2014